Your One Must-Read, Must-Think-About Book This Year.

Yes, it is possible that Malaysian Airlines Flight MH370 met with a tragic accident and fell into the sea on 8 March 2014 MYT.

However, the enigmatic circumstances of its sudden and near-silent disappearance demand that the world prepare for a terrifying yet plausible alternative.

The premise of this novel is that the plane (here portrayed as a fictional Flight 777) was hijacked by well-organized terrorists, is being weaponized, and will be used in an attack on civilization more dreadful than the attacks of 9/11.

Consider: the presumed hijacking came just before the third anniversary of Osama bin Ladin's death in May 2011. Rather than be complacent, we must anticipate a revenge action by his terrorist followers—to outdo 9/11 both in loss of life and breath-takingly spectacular planning and scope.

He will carefully pick the time and place of his assault—we must be ready. This novel (thought experiment) is an exercise in possibilities, without exhausting all, but enough to get us thinking.

An Entertaining Thriller

...but More Importantly:

a Riveting Thought Experiment—

Consider also: this enemy likes to use common means of transportation in his attacks on civilization, resulting in hundreds or thousands of casualties.

- World Trade Center NYC (26 Feb. 1993) — van bomb.

- *U.S.S. Cole* (attacked 12 October 2000—boat vs. warship).

- The well-planned 9/11/2001 attacks used civilian airliners.

- London ("7/7" in 2005) — underground trains and buses.

- Madrid (11 March 2004, or M-11) — passenger trains.

- Flight 777 (airliner) anyone?

This enemy has the means (an airliner), the motive (revenge, violent insanity), and plenty of opportune targets.

We must be prepared, and never, ever underestimate him.

We must out-think him, because he never stops obsessing about a world he hates, filled with happy, dancing, laughing, hard-working men, women, and children living normal, real lives.

He has only mass murder in his psychotic dreams for us.

Clocktower Books, San Diego Presents:

Vanished Flight 777

A Suspense Thriller & Thought Experiment Based on the True, Mysterious
Vanishing of Flight MH370—We Must Assume that a Horrific Terrorist Event
will soon be staged using the Hijacked Aircraft.

by

John T. Cullen

FILE UNDER: "OMINOUS" AND "MUST READ"

Clocktower Books
Exciting Reading for Avid Readers on the Web Since 1996
P. O. Box 600973
Grantville Station 92160
San Diego, California 92160-0973

E-Mail Contact: Editor/Publisher
editorial@clocktowerbooks.com

Look for other exciting fiction and nonfiction at the website of Clocktower Books: www.clocktowerbooks.com/. For more information, see the back of this book.

Dedicated

This Memorial Day 2014, to all in the West who have given their lives in the cause of liberty in a war we never chose, but which waged by a relentless and self-declared enemy of civilization, decency, and reason.

Secondly, my research has educated me to the plight of the Ilois or Chagossian people who were displaced from the Diego Garcia region by a cruel and pointless colonial mentality of U.K. and U.S. planners half a century ago. The world needs to understand their plight, and their need for a just outcome. We should return them to their rightful ancestral homes and graves in the region. They will be the best stewards and allies for peace and security we could ever ask for.

Finally, this Dedication embraces those, of all nationalities, who have suffered in connection with the disappearance of Malaysian Air Flight MH370. May a day soon arrive when we can at last truthfully bid them, and their loved ones, "Good Night, Malaysian 370."

Other Books by John T. Cullen Include:

More information available at the author's website

www.johntcullen.com/

Nonfiction from Clocktower Books

A Walk in Ancient Rome (Ancient History; First Authorized Edition 2015);

Dead Move: Kate Morgan & the Haunting Mystery of Coronado, 3rd Ed.;

And more…

Fiction (Novels) from Clocktower Books

The Spy's Daughter (historical fiction);

Doctor Night (suspense thriller in Ian Fleming tradition). Jack Dorsey of *Vanished Flight 777* (a prequel) years later becomes Jack Gray, hero of a coming series of Compass News thrillers set in a scary near future;

Lethal Journey (dramatization of *Dead Move* above, re: a notorious 1892 true crime at the Hotel del Coronado near San Diego);

Autumn of the Republic (20th Anniv. Edn of *The Generals of October*)—political thriller about a coup attempt during a 2nd Constitutional Convention or CON2;

Cymbalist Poems 1965-1975;

The Christmas Clock—dark, seasonal holiday fantasy—received a personal letter of praise from Ray Bradbury in January 2008;

And more…

Interested readers will find further information at the rear of this book, and on the websites of John T. Cullen and Clocktower Books.

www.clocktowerbooks.com/

Contents

Vanished Flight 777

Part One: Southeast Asia

1.   Flight Clock 00:00 and Ticking

For five glorious days, Jack Dorsey, his pregnant young wife Catherine, and several friends had vacationed on the beautiful beaches of the islands northwest of Malaysia in the Andaman Sea. Now, horrific events were about to get in the way, changing everything.

Jack Dorsey and his three Special Forces team members were part of a covert U.S. Army Reserve unit based near San Diego. They had just completed a four month hazardous mission in the Middle East, and were taking a much needed R&R break on their way back home. Their wives had flown overseas to join them.

Jack's last memory of the islands would be pleasant—of a humid, tropical late morning, sitting on a beach chair with a rum and coke, watching his wife Catherine and another woman running in the surf. The other was Marian Keaka. The two squealed and laughed as they playfully kicked water at each other. Captain Robert Keaka sat near Jack, holding a margarita, and smiling happily as he watched the fun. He and Jack exchanged pleased glances. It was good to unwind, forget battle, and be with loved ones. Not far up the beach were four other members of the group— two Special Forces master sergeants and their wives. They grinned lazily and regarded the antics of Catherine and Marian over the rims of mai tai and margarita glasses.

Catherine, six months pregnant, came chugging up the sand. She was a compact, athletic woman, and looked especially pretty at this point in her pregnancy. "You look funny with that orange stuff on your nose," she told Jack.

"Laugh all you want. When your nose is peeling on the flight home, you'll wish you followed my advice."

Catherine—shapely, brunette verging on blonde, wearing a black and orange bikini—lowered herself on the big beach towel near Jack and reached for a coconut containing iced lemonade. She sipped from a straw.

Jack lowered himself onto the towel and sat directly before her. She squinted up at him with blue-gray eyes. He rubbed some of the sun-goop from his nose onto his finger, and dabbed her nose and upper lip with it.

A voice called from nearby. "Hey, love birds, let's go have lunch." It was Marian Keaka, wife of the other officer along with the group—Robert Keaka. Both were native Hawai'ians who had transplanted to Southern California with Robert's military contractor engineering job. Marian, who had thick, long, glossy black hair, full reddened lips, and flashing dark eyes, regarded her friends fondly. "You two are still like newly weds."

Jack took Catherine's face between his palms and kissed her. "We just haven't had time to get over it yet."

Catherine closed her eyes and sought Jack's tongue with hers. He had never met a woman like her. They'd been married nearly two years now, yet every day with her was like their honeymoon continued. She was a quiet person, but with the same intense feelings toward her husband. They had found each other during his active duty travels. She was an Arizona girl, happy to have a horse and some range—of which Jack's quietly well-to-do family in San Diego County had plenty. They'd pledged total loyalty to the end, and each meant it.

"I have to count your freckles again," he said softly.

"I think they are still all there," she said a bit ruefully. She was self-conscious about the sprinkling of blunt little orange stains around her small nose. Jack described himself as a Freckles Man— they drove him crazy in a woman, especially if she had them "all over" as she'd admitted innocently when they first met.

"Can you believe it," Robert called out. "Pupu Platter. These people know how to party." He referred to *pupu*, a Hawai'ian buffet or hors d'oeuvre including chicken, tempura vegetables, cubed raw fish, and other delectables. Robert, a captain in the army reserve like Jack, had the rather typical lean, wiry physique of someone who exercised a great deal. They were lean and wiry men—Jack; Robert; Sergeant Ben Latoni of Poughkeepsie, New York; and Sergeant Ray Marston of St. Louis, Missouri. The Latonis were Italian-American, while the Marstons were African-American.

The four had returned lean, hungry, and somewhat spooked from a dangerous mission with U.S. Navy SEALS. In past days, their Special Forces unit had trained with a SEAL (SEa, Air, Land) unit in Coronado, in exchange for which the same unit of SEALs had trained with them at a secret U.S. Army jungle base in Panama. Your mission was not something you wanted to tell your wife and children about—unconventional warfare. Catherine had no idea that Jack belonged to a shadowy group, a fleeting, phantom Temporary Duty (TDY) on paper, for pay purposes only, masquerading as a weather station in the Aleutian Islands. Jack had never been to the Aleutians, nor did a weather station by that designation exist. The wives understood all this, and appreciated it. "I don't want to know," Catherine had said with a sigh more than once. Jack's reply had been: "And that's the best way to leave it."

She had regarded him with those serious gray-blue eyes, amid pale skin and freckles, and said: "I married you knowing you'd be off doing all sorts of who knows what."

He'd been barbecuing in back of their ranch in Temecula, San Diego at the time, and flipped a rack of ribs with a little extra emphasis. "A little of the what, and easy on the who knows."

Holding her drink, she'd winked at him. "All you need is a pirate patch over one eye."

"And a parrot," he'd said. "And you would have to wear a bandanna."

"A banana? Yo ho ho, a pirate's wife am I." She giggled and they both laughed.

That was now nearly two years ago and over 10,000 miles away. This was a lovely tropical beach on the Kedah peninsula of Malaysia, not far from the Thai border on the Sea of Andaman.

Jack now rose, offering his hand. She sprang up, taking his hand, and they ran together across the white sand toward a cluster of huts thatched with palm fronds at the edge of a jungle. Rising out of the jungle were the dark red roof tiles of an exclusive hotel. Funding for this vacation came largely from a variety of financial pots stirred by secret U.S. government agencies. Jack had kicked in an extra day's stay from his pocket, being the only really wealthy member of UNCON667. For obscure reasons, they were also known as Team Gray.

The unseen eyes of Uncle Sam followed Team Gray everywhere they went. When you were in Jack Dorsey's line of work, you were always required to let the host country embassy know your whereabouts, in case of some crisis. Of course, you notified them that you were a tourist, innocently traveling on such and such passport, and wanted to check the status of the necessary inoculations. Which told the local CIA team what they needed to know, and you heard nothing more from them—except this would all change in a matter of hours as Flight 777 took to the air.

It was about bonding. The four men had faced bullets, IEDs, and other hazards on their recent mission. They had witnessed some horrific things, best left behind, though each of them had on occasion awakened on the floor after suddenly screaming in the middle of the night and flying out of bed in a tangle of sheets. The wives became as used to it as might be possible, which was partly 'never'. Maybe not used to it, as Catherine told Jack one night while soothing him as he sat sweating and breathing hard on the floor, and she stroked his short-cropped head with a cool washcloth, over and over again, with the most gentle and loving imaginable touch. Maybe not used to it, but you adapt to almost anything. Catherine never asked questions, and Jack never told her. It was, he thought, the best gift he could give her—not knowing what he had seen and done. And most of it was, as people in the profession said, hours and days of utter boredom punctuated by moments of sheer terror. That was why you had Rest & Relaxation (R&R) in distant, out of the way places like this to draw a mental line between yourself and your history. Having your loved one along was a good, added lubricant to ease the transition.

It was all about bonding, as the eight persons dining on pupu to the tunes of island music understood at an unspoken level. The men were bonded by their experiences, and the women were bonded by being their most important contact with the real, normal world outside of war. This was why what happened a day later was so devastating to the six who remained on the ground when Flight 777 took off. And why the mission to find—or later, recover; and ultimately, to uncover—Flight 777 was a personal one for the three remaining men.

After lunch, a comfortable jitney specially rented for the occasion drove the eight to a modest but clean ferry boat. This motor vessel took them, chugging across the foamy waters of the Andaman Sea, to the larger island of Langkawi, from whose smaller international airport they boarded a twin-engine AirAsia Airbus passenger jet to the main international airport at Kuala Lumpur.

"It's kind of good to be back in civilization," Robert Keaka said as he stood with one arm around his wife Marian. They were in the huge, modern halls of KUL, as thousands of persons milled about.

"I know what you mean," Jack said. He held Catherine's hand as they stood waiting with their carry on bags. "Kind of overwhelming, but in a good way."

"Bring it on," said Ray Marston, while Ben Latoni grinned.

They did not need to describe what they felt. Civilization washed round them, the way the tides of the sea do around a toothy, kelp-strewn shore, and renew it. The noise, the sheer pressure of millions of people and their activities, would complete the R&R as much as possible—so they expected, before anyone knew what was coming next.

By 11:30 p.m. Kuala Lumpur time (eight hours ahead of Greenwich Mean Time or Coordinated Universal Time), Marian and Robert Keaka had said their goodbyes and boarded the 777 200ER bound for Beijing. They were going to meet Marian's sister and husband for a further sightseeing vacation in China's capital city, before returning to Southern California a week later. Jack's last view of them was of Robert's studious, calm face with his scholarly eyeglasses and satisfied, domestic smile, and Marian's cheerful hugs with the women of the group.

Jack was happy for Robert and Marian. He was ready to spend some R&R on his ranch in Temecula, watching Catherine ride around on her mare Gustava. Also along would be the new foal, Justina. It was kind of all in synch, since Catherine was due to give birth in another twelve weeks. Jack had family business to tend to, in addition to which he and Catherine had already set aside a room in the spacious house for a nursery. He held her tightly and lovingly, sometimes straying a hand over her belly and coincidentally meeting her hand there.

The other three couples all had children already. Robert and Marian had two teenagers attending school in Honolulu. Ray and his wife Latrice Marston had two teenage boys staying with her family in St. Louis, Missouri; while Ben Latoni and his wife Shelley had a boy and two girls, aged six, seven, and nine, in upstate New York.

By midnight, Flight 777 was buttoned up and ready to leave the gate.

Jack and Catherine joined their friends in walking out of the terminal to catch a jitney for their east-bound flight to Manila, Honolulu, and Los Angeles.

They could see the tall tail fin of the Boeing 777 as it crawled past the large plate glass windows of the terminal. The roof had spectacular waves of glass, reinforced with steel trusses, that brought in daylight and, now, starlight. The night outside was warm and clear.

"It will be so nice to get home," Catherine said. "I am sure Janet has been feeding Gustava and the baby." She meant the foal.

"You worry too much, mommy."

"I am a mommy. Or about to be. I'm just starting to practice being worried."

He rubbed her back, feeling the delightful curves of her dry skin under the thin cotton of her colorful tropical dress.

By half past midnight, the three USA-bound couples were in the boarding area of their Lufthansa flight, waiting as the quietly efficient Germans in their dark blue uniforms made all the standard preparations. It would be a full flight to Manila, and the air crew were fully staffed.

At 00:41, or forty-one minutes past midnight, Malaysian Airlines Flight 777 thundered into the sky on its powerful twin engines. It was a healthy, robust scene as the huge machine, with nearly 250 passengers on board, headed toward the stars.

Zero Hour of the Flight Clock for Flight 777 had just come and gone. The historic flight into mystery and oblivion had begun, though nobody as yet had any idea of the enigma unfolding.

2. Manila Turn-About

The flight from Kuala Lumpur International Airport (KUL) to Manila was uneventful, and packed. The Lufthansa Airbus thundered quietly and safely through the skies over the South China Sea on its way to the Philippines.

The Team Gray did not get to sit together, but near each other, probably by design. On domestic flights, they were always known to the flight crew and on-board sky marshals. Jack usually traveled under orders, and someone always knew where he sat, what he did, and whether he needed backup or a call back to action.

Catherine had a window seat, with Jack often bending across her lap to peer outside at passing cities filled with light. Sometimes they pressed their heads together, and kissed.

"I missed you so," she said as she held her left arm around his back, and rubbed his forearm (resting on the window) with her right hand.

Ben Latoni and his blonde wife sat two seats behind, jammed in the middle of a wide row, while Ray Marston and his attractive wife sat across the aisle.

The flight to Ninoy Aquino International in Manila took just under four hours. It was a subdued flight, with the lights dimmed. Jack and Catherine had dozed off by the time the great plane began its descent. He was feeling the effects of days of sunshine and running around, while Catherine slept peacefully with her head resting on his chest, and one hand raised to his collar bone as if it were her pillow at home. As he woke up, Jack kissed her forehead and hair lightly, inhaling her fragrance. It would be good to spend time together on the ranch back in San Diego County.

As he woke, Jack felt a bit muzzy and disoriented. He had to remind himself of his surroundings and of his immediate past. Yes, he'd been on the ground in the Middle East with nearly a dozen other members of Team Gray. Two were now still traveling with him after Robert Keaka had split off, bound with his wife for China. After several men had headed for duty stations—in Europe and elsewhere—only Jack, Ben, and Ray were still together.

Catherine sighed in her sleep and hugged Jack tightly. It was a sigh of utter happiness, and a smile played around her lips. He hugged her gently to him as the plane landed.

The expectation was that they would lay over in Manila for an hour, during which time the Honolulu-bound passengers would remain in their seats. Some local residents would get off, and some new passengers bound for the U.S.A. would board.

The progress of events did not turn out that way.

As he sat waiting in the still aircraft, with Catherine resting on his chest and ground crew driving around below in vehicles with flashing lights, a female cabin crew member tapped Jack on the shoulder. "Mr. Dorsey," she said in barely accented English. She was a blonde in her upper 30s, with incipient crow's feet that blended gracefully with moderate make-up. "I have an important message for you from the Captain."

"Oh?" Alarm bells went off in Jack's head.

"Will you come with me, Mr. Dorsey?"

"Yes. Hang on a moment." Shifting his body, he gently eased Catherine into her seat.

"Baby?" Catherine woke briefly and reached for him with mild, confused anxiety. "Jack?"

"I'm here, sweetheart. I have to go see the captain about something. You go right on sleeping, okay? I'll be right back."

As he made his way to the front, he noticed that Ben Latoni and Ray Marston were also being summoned out of their seats.

As the men blended into a file together, Ray said: "Looks like an excuse to stretch our legs."

"I don't like the looks of this," Ben said. He was shorter than Ray, and more of a compact tank of a guy, whereas Ray Marston was tall and thin, and carried himself with the loose-limbed amble of a basketball player.

As the only officer among them, Jack was the leader. The other two men were senior NCOs, each quite accomplished in his own realm. In fact, each of the other two men was on a list for Warrant Officer. They shared equanimity, more than most places in the military. Theirs was an occupation where you did not play rank, and anyone's life could depend on another man's total trust.

The boarding port was open. Lights and airport smells drifted in, along with the straggling of passengers pulling wheeled luggage and looking suitably confused, while a half dozen male and female cabin attendants in jaunty blue uniforms welcomed them.

Jack, followed by Ben and Ray, made his way past them to the cockpit. There, two pilots in dark uniforms, distinguished by the stripes on their sleeves, welcomed them. The tall, dark-haired captain was a Herr Unterstein or something—Jack could not quite make out his name tag in the dim light, nor understand his slightly accented, rapid speech.

"I have been instructed by the local authorities to relay a message to you from your embassy," said Captain Unterstein. "You are urgently required to deplane here now and see a local consular official about your inoculations."

"Oh, is there something wrong?" Jack said—suddenly weary, because this did not sound like anything he wanted to hear.

"No, they said everything is in order, but you must see the consular official immediately. I have been instructed that you will most likely not be on board with us when we take off. I regret this very much."

"Thank you," Jack said. He turned. "Guys, bad news."

"Aw fer," began Ben, and Ray seconded "I can't believe it."

"Our inoculations. You know the drill."

They had just long enough to say goodbye to their wives, who would be flying on alone to Honolulu and then Los Angeles, with further stops as warranted. Catherine was a grown woman and he need not worry that she'd lose her way finding San Diego. Still, Jack felt a feeling of chagrin, deepened only by a sense of apprehension. What could possibly be so important that he and Team Gray were yanked from a civilian flight while off duty and on civilian travel?

After a long, tender, desperate hug with Catherine, Jack grabbed his carry-on bag and joined the other two men as they walked down the rubberized, dully rumbling corridor to the boarding port, then across the long bridge and into the terminal.

Like all international airport terminals at night, anywhere in the world, Ninoy Aquino was brightly lit, clean, and boringly modern. That was Jack's recurring opinion, having passed through most of the world's major airports, usually on duty—often under cover, and never for a pleasant reason. He had no doubt that this was happening for some highly unpleasant reason. The other two men knew as much in their hearts. And they would not be disappointed. Shocked, yes—but not surprised.

The consular official who met them was an Asian-American from San Francisco named Charles Unaga. He wore a dark suit, white shirt, and red tie, and showed his identification. "Sorry to pull you guys."

"We get used to it," Ray Marston said. "Not that we like it."

Unaga handed them fresh tickets. "You are on duty, and going back to Kuala Lumpur. There has been an event."

"Here it comes," Ben Latoni said. "What happened?"

"I'm not privy to much info on this," Unaga said, "but Malaysia is missing a passenger jet, and I can only assume that someone knows something suspicious."

Jack's first question was: "Terrorists?"

Unaga shrugged. "You will be briefed when you hit the ground back at KUL. I have no idea. It's just breaking in the news around the world. You watch ten minutes of CNN and you'll know as much as I do."

"You're just the messenger," Ray said.

"We'll forgive you," Ben said.

"Can you lead us to our flight?" Jack said.

Unaga signaled to a local skycap, who pulled up in a large golf cart looking vehicle. "At least you get to ride in style," Charlie Unaga said soothingly. He accompanied the three men to a remote runway under fresh air and open, starry skies, where a U.S. Air Force C-21 passenger jet was just being serviced for take-off.

"You're lucky guys," Charlie Unaga said. "You are bumping several pissed off admirals who will have to take the next hop."

"My heart grieves," Jack said. There were no admirals in sight as he and the other men clambered up the steel stairs. A U.S. Air Force sergeant in flight blues saluted them on board and started buttoning up the hatch. Outside, Philippine ground crew hauled the steps away, driving a tractor with flashing orange lights.

The C-21 is an older military equivalent of the Lear Jet 35A business aircraft. Jack and his men knew the type well. The C-21, painted gray with subdued USAF markings, can function as a cargo lift, passenger jet, or air ambulance. It is a sleek jet, with relatively short wings, and two powerful turbofan engines tucked close to the fuselage, high aft of the wings. The craft is forward-thrust in design, with a relatively short, lifted T-configured tail section. As a passenger jet, it can haul up to eight passengers, space available, traveling on orders. As an air ambulance, it can evacuate half a dozen walking wounded, or two severe casualties, accompanied by up to three medical technicians, doctors, or flight nurses.

The particular model in which Jack, Ben, and Ray presently took off had a look of worn comfort, almost luxury. The aircraft type had been in service for over thirty years, and was being phased out. Like many workhorse military aircraft, it smelled of rubber, oil, and coffee.

Jack and his team wasted no time complaining. This was what they had signed up for.

"Must be something exceptionally bad," Ray ventured as they sat in the semi-dark, heading back the way they had just come.

Jack put his feet up on his bag. "I don't know about you guys, but I'm going to catch up on sack time. Never know when or if we get to sleep again."

"Wise words," Ben agreed.

They had the plane all to themselves. One of the pilots came aft to introduce himself—an Air National Guard colonel from Texas, very solicitous and professional. Other than that, they had a peaceful flight unwinding the four hours they had earlier traveled.

At one point, the cabin staff sergeant came forward to check on them. No, he said, they did not have a working satellite news feed. The system was down. Which was just as well, Jack thought as he drifted off into a torpid sleep.

In Kuala Lumpur, it was noon when the C-21 touched down. It was a slightly overcast, muggy tropical day with light showers. A white Mercedes picked up Jack and his two companions and took them to a U.S. Consulate facility just off the airport grounds in Kuala Lumpur.

Jack felt a mix of regret and rested as they drove onto the consulate grounds. Local staff opened the doors and carried their luggage. They were escorted into a warren of offices, and met their new duty supervisor—Colonel Lew Minchao, a Filipino-American U.S. Air Force officer, wearing casual civilian clothing—or, in the case of a man of his stature, the closest thing to casual being the absence of a necktie and the unbuttoning of his collar. His khaki trousers, brown suede shoes, and crisp white shirt could be converted to business attire with the addition of a tie and a jacket, and the buttoning of that collar (which was in fact button-down).

"Gentlemen," said Minchao heartily, as he shook each man's hand. They were in a space that looked more like a garage or a metal shed than an office, especially a high ranking officer's. As the men grabbed whatever half-broken seats they could, forming a semi-circle, Minchao began their briefing. As he spoke, two oddly military looking civilian U.S. staff wheeled in a television on a metal rack. "We're kind of primitive here," Minchao said. "Pardon the mess, but we are rushing to set up for business. So have you seen the news?"

Jack shook his head. "No, sir. We actually slept all the way back here. No tube on board the ferry plane."

Minchao nodded. "Okay. I can give you the short sermon real quick, because there is little that we know as yet. Before I do, let me inform you that we are currently under the technical command of our theater commander higher up, but operationally we are working for and with some spooks, maybe CIA. Everything we say and do here is top secret, purple, and beyond. Got that?"

"Yessir," the three men echoed.

"You men are officially on orders, on duty, and subject to the usual UCMJ and protocols. In addition, I can tell you that this operation has high visibility in Washington D.C. as well as the Pentagon. We all keep our noses clean, yes?"

"Yessir."

"Here's the run-down as far as we know. What the news won't tell you is that the United States and our allies around the world have had serious intel that something was going to transpire involving a large passenger aircraft. Now this is nothing new. Last decade, the Haters were going to hijack a dozen jet liners and crash them all at once on their way to the U.S.A., but all they managed was one shoe bomber and one underwear creature. This pathetic stuff goes on constantly. And you are asking—why you? Couple of reasons. For starters, one of your team members is missing on that flight, along with his wife: Robert and Marian Keaka."

"Oh no," Jack said, echoed by his companions. He felt a wrench in his gut, like battery acid. They'd all just been together and so happy. Jack recalled sitting on a beach chair just two days ago, with a drink in his hand, watching Catherine and Marian frolicking in the surf. And now this.

"We have grabbed what traveling specialists we could, and you were among the handiest personnel who had the bad luck to be traveling through southeast Asian air space. You know how it is." Minchao stood with his back to a large table, resting his butt on it. "The powers on high do not know us personally. We are merely ciphers and letters of the alphabet. When shiitake goes down, they pull any rabbit that comes out of the hat. You, gentlemen, are among those rabbits, so welcome to Operation Mike Alpha Papa, Missing Air Plane, or MAP for short. We'll make up a more clever name tomorrow. Our intelligence network around the world was on a heightened alert status, which bumps things up for lots of people, but lots of times it's a false alarm and we go back to normal. And yes, in case you are wondering, I am a retired Air Force officer, Reservist like you are, and double dipping with the Foreign Service here in Malaysia—at our embassy, to be specific. I do some consulting work with the CIA and other intelligence agencies, but I will not repeat what I just said. I only emphasize how sensitive your mission here is. Because" (he paused for emphasis, looking at each of them) "if we need to send guys into harm's way, you will be the first to go."

"Any idea what kind of mission that might be?" Jack asked. At last, Minchao was homing in on something that Jack could sink his teeth into. The missing friends—Robert and Marian—was a horrible enough situation, and a motivator for sure.

Minchao said: "We are hoping, guys, that we'll have the opportunity for a rescue operation. We have other units on the way, but you will be first in, best briefed, and ready to take point when others arrive. I might as well tell you, also, that some of those may be civilian contractors, just so you know."

Jack and his two companions made faces. On the one hand, most of the civilians you met in the field were ex-military, which gave you points to relate on. Some had attitudes because they were getting at least ten times the pay, worked for civilian black operations firms, and were immune from military protocol.

"That all said," Minchao continued, "this is going to be tedious, so please bear with me. I'll give you the known sequence of events so far. We're using several time reference frames.

"Flight time refers to the clock on board the missing 777, starting at 00:00 hours as she took off at 41 minutes after midnight last night.

"Malaysia Standard Time or MYT refers to local time in Kuala Lumpur.

"Greenwich Mean Time (GMT) is eight hours behind MYT, along with another modern standard, Coordinated Universal Time.

"Flight 777 took off from KUL at 00:41 a.m. MYT. As you know, the Keakas were supposed to fly across Vietnamese airspace into mainland China airspace to land at Beijing on a routine flight. Nothing out of the ordinary.

"However, at 41 minutes after midnight, 8 March MYT—that is 16:41 or 4:41 p.m. in the afternoon of March 7 in the London area—Flight 777 lifted off from KUL (Kuala Lumpur International Airport). Let's call that Flight Clock 00:00.

"Flight Clock 00:20, or twenty minutes later (1:01 a.m. MYT) the crew confirmed with the control tower at KUL that they have reached their cruising altitude of 35,000 feet (11,000 meters).

"Flight clock 00:26, or 1:07 a.m. MYT—twenty-six minutes into the flight, the crew confirms their 35,000 foot cruising altitude as is normal. This turns out to be the last ACARS (Aircraft Communications Addressing and Reporting System) transmission received at KUL. That is, as you know, an automated networked system for relaying flight status information, which takes some of the manual workload off cockpit crew.

"Flight Clock 00:38, thirty-eight minutes into the flight, at 1:19 a.m. MYT—we have the last Malaysian Air Traffic Control (ATC) voice communication with the aircraft. This was Malaysia telling the plane to switch its conversation over to Vietnam for the handshake and takeover. The plane is now approaching halfway between Malaysia and Ho Chi Minh City ATC over the Gulf of Thailand. At this time, the Vietnamese ATC should smoothly take over from their Malaysian counterparts.

"Flight Clock 00:40, forty minutes into the flight, at 1:21 a.m. MYT, we have a last secondary radar or transponder contact at 6°55'15"N 103°34'43"E northeast of Penang. Penang is in Peninsular Malaysia south of the Thailand border."

Jack interrupted: "We were on vacation not far from there."

Minchao acknowledged with a nod, and continued: "Flight Time 00:40—(01:21 KUL) last secondary radar or transponder contact at a location over the Gulf of Thailand, en route to Vietnam, where apparently the aircraft made a sharp left or westward turn for no explicable reason."

"We would have just gotten into the air on our way to Manila," Ray said.

Again, Minchao acknowledged, apparently glad he had their attention and that they were drawing connections. "Okay, so Flight Clock 00:41 ATC loses contact with transponder and ADS-B (Automatic Dependent Surveillance Broadcast) system. This is another automated flight control system, whereby the aircraft checks its location automatically with a satellite and ground network. Malaysia is aware of the situation, but Vietnam picks up the ball. Nine minutes go by, during which Vietnam is totally unable to pick up contact with the aircraft."

Minchao paused and looked at the three men. "We now know this is because the aircraft made a sharp, unplanned western or left turn.

"Flight Clock 00:49—forty-nine minutes into the flight, or nearly an hour, at 01:30 MYT—ATC in Ho Chi Minh City requests another aircraft to make voice contact. They do this, but there is nothing to be heard but mumbling and radio static. However, there is no alarm or may day distress signal. You understand that now we are into unknown territory, so to speak. Nobody knows what is going on with the aircraft."

As Minchao spoke, he was interrupted by a young woman in a dark jogging suit, a brunette who looked Caucasian and, to Jack's eye, probably on the local U.S. staff. The young woman brought a folded message, which she handed to Minchao and then quickly left. Minchao paused to open the several folded sheets of paper and read. He said: "Gentlemen, we have new intelligence. Apparently, there were at least three suspicious individuals on board Flight 777. Two were Iranian nationals flying with stolen European passports."

"That's not suspicious," Ben said.

"Not at all," Ray seconded.

"Why am I not surprised?" Jack said.

"And this," Minchao added: "There was another passenger of unknown nature who is deemed suspicious. So we have at least three possible terrorists on board, possibly hijackers. It may be nothing, but we'll be receiving all incoming traffic of this nature on a real time basis as our sources acquire it."

"How many persons on board?" Jack asked.

"There were 229 passengers and 12 flight crew, for a total of 241," Minchao said. He continued: "The last words from Malaysian Flight 777 were spoken by the pilots at 01:19 a.m. (Flight Clock 00:47) when they routinely informed the Kuala Lumpur ATC to the effect: *Good Night, Malaysian Air*[1]. That is still routine, or at least it sounds so. But something happens in the next ten minutes."

"Hijack," Jack guessed.

"Quite possibly," Minchao said. "Remember, we are speculating. Who knows, in our most fantastic dreams, this could all turn out to be a misunderstanding and we can all go home. Or the plane simply crashed during the night, and it becomes a recovery operation—and not so much of a mystery anymore.

"Okay, so at this point the Malaysians and/or the Vietnamese put out a kind of all points bulletin to their equivalents in Singapore, Hong Kong, Phnom Penh, and other ATC network nodes for hundreds of miles around, asking for a possible fix on the missing aircraft. Nobody spots anything.

"Flight Clock 00:56—01:37 a.m. MYT—the plane fails to exchange its standard, half-hour ACARS data transmission.

"Flight Clock 00:57—01:38 a.m. MYT—Ho Chi Minh contacts Kuala Lumpur to officially notify them that they have not established contact including verbal conversation. A series of contacts between the two ATCs include potentially misunderstood or erroneous information that causes delays in the assessment that Flight 777 has effectively vanished."

"Wow. Strong stuff," Jack said.

---

[1] In the true life case, actually "Good night Malaysian three seven zero."

"And then," Minchao said, "get this. Flight Clock 01:34, or nearly an hour later, Malaysian military radars near Penang pick up a contact 200 miles (320 km) northwest of their position at 6°49′38″N 97°43′15″E. On this bearing, the aircraft is still in the air and heading due west from its planned handshake position halfway to Ho Chi Minh City.

"Flight Clock 01:41—02:22 a.m. MYT—still exchanging ACARS pings with the Inmarsat-3 F1 satellite system. That means the flight is still in the air.

"Flight Clock 05:49—06:30 MYT and close to daybreak in the region—just over five hours after departure, official word that Flight 777 failed to reach Beijing as scheduled.

"Flight Clock 06:43—(07:24 MYT) we have official word from Malaysia Airlines that the flight is missing. By now, gentlemen, our own regional intelligence services have picked up the story, and we radioed ahead to Manila to get you guys back here—just in case.

"Flight Clock 07:30, or 08:11 MYT, we have the last successful automated handshake with Inmarsat-3 F1 satellite. This is a very simple, rudimentary, three point communication between machines in which the first machine says Synchronize (SYN), the responding machine says Synchronize + Acknowledge (SYN-ACK), and the first machine responds Acknowledged (ACK), ending the conversation or handshake.

"Oddly, at Flight Clock 07:38 (08:19 MYT), there is an unscheduled, inexplicable partial handshake transmitted by the aircraft.

"Flight Clock 08:34 (09:15 MYT) or well over eight hours into the flight, Inmarsat makes another scheduled attempt at a handshake, which goes unanswered. Most likely, the plane is down somewhere by now, and its systems have been disabled. We can't say if that would include the black box flight recorder systems. That's all we know right now, gentlemen."

"How far could the plane have flown?" Ben asked.

"Good question. Bear in mind that she was only partially fueled, enough to reach Beijing, which would require about sixty percent of full fuel capacity. You're not going to fly a plane with more fuel on board than you need. You want to conserve the fuel needed to carry the fuel. We have to assume that the plane dropped into the water at some point after this."

"Or landed?" Jack asked.

"Landed—but where? And why?" Minchao looked around. "Those are the questions we are going to answer. You men will stay around my operational headquarters here until future notice. Bear in mind that we are on consular ground, which is not quite embassy status, but we are conducting sensitive intelligence operations on foreign soil. Don't go cruising off to any local bars or hamburger joints, okay?" The colonel managed a crisp, cold little grin, which broke the tension in the room a bit.

Aides brought in coffee and pastries.

As the men milled around, stretching their legs, Jack spoke with Minchao. "Other than warming seats, what do you need for us to do? Like all geniuses, we get bored easily."

"Not to worry, Captain. We'll keep you busy. I want you and your men to help us with scenarios. You'll have a secure phone and access to U.S. military and diplomatic channels as needed. I want you to form your own guess as to what is going on. Fair enough?"

"Sounds like a fun game, if only it were a game."

"I understand you have friends on board."

"Yes, we do. It's no game." Jack was only glad that Catherine and the other wives would be safely back in the United States by now. As worried as he was about Bob and Marian, the last thing he needed was to be out of his mind with worry over the woman he loved. His sister and brother in law back at the ranch would take good care of her as always, and Catherine could concentrate peacefully on her approaching due date with motherhood.

Minchao told Jack privately later that evening: "Jack, just a heads up. This situation is getting more serious all the time. I think we'll be evacuated to Diego Garcia soon, to get on our own turf."

"For operational freedom?"

"Yeah. The locals are incredibly sensitive. This situation looks bad for them, mainly because it appears they were slow on the uptake. I would argue either way, but they'll be tried in the news media. That's now this always works."

"Colonel, you're not going to let them jam us together with some mercenaries, are you?"

"I'll do my best to keep all the stacks of folks separate, Jack. I can't promise you anything, but I'll do what I can."

Jack knew that he'd have a tough time acting as a military commander with mercenary troops. It was like water and oil as far as he was concerned—the two did not mix. "Thanks. Will you be coming with us to Diego Garcia?"

Minchao shrugged. "No idea. This is now a world wide operation by our government."

Jack felt startled. "I thought we were backing the locals up."

"It's potentially bigger than that, Jack. We have to keep it low to the ground, but there may be a lot more at stake than Malaysian pride, or even the 241 people on board."

Jack regarded the table to one side of him, which he and his team had taken over. This was their operational theater right now— a table with a map, a phone, some rulers and other measuring devices, and a lot of colored markers. "We are going to operate on the assumption that the aircraft was hijacked."

Minchao nodded. "That's fine. There are already search and rescue operations going on in the Andaman Sea and the Indian Ocean."

"Fine. We'll let them operate on the assumption the plane went down in a horrible accident."

"It would actually be simpler if that were the case."

"Yeah; then it would be an issue for Boeing engineers to resolve—and we could go home." His tone had yearning in it.

"Something tells me this is not going to be that easy."

"Sure," Jack said. "We have to try all the angles. If someone were to hijack the plane, you'd think we'd have some word already. Like if they did it for money, or to get free passage to somewhere."

"Or a ransom demand."

"Whatever. Arab and/or Muslim terrorists come to mind."

"Malaysia is a predominantly Muslim nation. The pilots and many of the passengers and flight crew were Muslims. Doesn't quite make sense, does it?"

Jack shook his head. "Unless we are dealing with one group against another, like Sunni and Shi'a or something of that kind. That's beyond my pay grade."

"And mine," Minchao said. "Maybe our command will relieve us, bring smart people in to solve the case, and send us home, huh?"

"As much as it hurts my pride, I'd welcome the relief."

After his conversation with Minchao, Jack rejoined Ben and Ray. He knew his men. These two guys were more about action than theory. "Guys," he told them, "I think you should plan for a ground operation. Figure out equipment, see what you can steal or otherwise procure from U.S. resources without anyone noticing, and do a lot of pushups."

"And you?" Ray said. "You're gonna push colored crayons all over that map?"

"Not for long, I hope. I see us all out yomping before long." Yomping is the U.K. Royal Marines' slang for marching long distances with heavy packs—the most soldierly of all soldierly ordeals and rites of passage. Where the term originated would be anyone's guess, but Jack imagined it was related to the word 'jumping' in some obscure English dialect, either with parachuting in mind, or else hopping over gopher holes along the way.

Over the next few days, Jack let Ben and Ray occupy themselves as they wished. That kept them out of his hair, and made them feel wanted. On the side, he watched with pleasure as a small pile of tactical equipment started to build up, starting with items like flares and rations they had requisitioned from embassy Marine Corps supplies. Of primary concern was their weaponry, an area in which each man could follow his preferences, but there were standard items to quickly fall back on like the 9 mm Glock with plenty of spare rounds, and some variation of the ever-present M-16. Beyond that, each man got to choose his favorite weapons.

Jack meanwhile occupied himself with watching the news and tracking down leads. Every smallest detail could count for something huge. He had two computers running at the far edge of the big table, each with a separate English-language news broadcast.

There appeared to be a constant stream of often contradictory information in the news. One moment, the plane was said to have crashed in the sea. The next moment, there was a ping somewhere or a weak signal from underwater.

A fisherman in the South China Sea had reported a burning object in the sky, which he took to be Flight 777 going down in flames.

Another individual reported a similar object near Hong Kong.

Both of those would be way east of the position and vector heading last reported for Flight 777.

Jack had Ben and Ray contact various embassies in the region, whose officials contacted local universities, and within a day, Jack was reasonably certain that those flaming objects had actually been meteors—objects from space, entering the atmosphere and burning up, sometimes spectacularly. They were popularly known as shooting stars, and had been associated with all sorts of baleful cosmic portents since ancient times.

There was one report that kept Jack's attention, however. A fisherman in the Maldives had reported seeing a Malaysia Airlines passenger jet flying overhead at a very low altitude. Fishermen, especially captains handling relatively sophisticated electronic equipment, were not fools. The news story of Flight 777 was all over the world by now, reaching into every corner of the globe— including the tiny satellite-fed receivers on board a pitching boat in the middle of the Indian Ocean. The captain's comment, carried on the news media, was that the plane was clearly visible, flying so low over the water as to make the fisherman wonder if the pilots were out of their minds. They had never seen anything like it. And, clearly visible on the fuselage, were the distinctive red on white fleet colors of Malaysian Airlines.

Something about this story festered in Jack's thoughts.

He discussed it with Minchao. "If this plane was taken—rather than crashed or lost at sea—someone must have had quite a sophisticated plan of operation."

"And purpose, if you're right."

"I am developing a theory, Colonel."

"I'm all ears."

Jack gesticulated over his map, which consisted of large sheets of computer-generated printouts in black and white, taped together. It had started out as a map of Southeast Asia including Singapore and Malaysia, and soon grown to include a swath of earth and sea extending from the South China Sea in the east, to as far north as the Himalaya Mountains north of India, and the entire Indian Ocean including the eastern half of Africa. More recently, Jack had tacked on portions to represent Western Asia (the Middle East) and southern Europe. He was just working on adding the entire Mediterranean.

"Wow, ambitious," Minchao added as he surveyed the map.

"I am operating on the theory that the plane was hijacked, and flown westward. That rules out Australia, Singapore, Southeast Asia, and the Philippines."

Minchao was not entirely convinced. "Well, half the world is searching the Indian Ocean now. They interpolated the plane's fuel capacity, and figured out a range that puts it along an arc—a few hundred miles west of Australia. There is a huge tropical storm, category five, raging there right now in fact. Nobody figures it could have been flown north along that hypothetical arc into Iran, or Afghanistan, or Pakistan. So your point is what, Jack?"

"There can be as many theories as there are stars in the sky or points on this map, Colonel. I'm going to run with my gut feeling that a fishing boat captain in the Indian Ocean actually, really, and truly did see our plane cruising along over the ocean at one to three thousand feet altitude. That particular Maldives sighting is admittedly a single coordinate, but it is the only one we have. There was another claim, later in the day, which we are discounting. The fisherman's story doesn't sound like a lie or delusion. It's too detailed and exact. Let's run with that assumption for now."

"That would mean that the plane was taken for a reason."

"Exactly. We have search and rescue going on. Let's run with the opposite assumption—a purposeful hijack. The Maldives are halfway across the Indian Ocean on a westward path toward Africa. The Maldives Archipelago or island chain is just a few hundred miles north of Diego Garcia, our leased home on British islands in the Indian Ocean. Our island aircraft carrier, so to speak.

"If the plane really did pass over the Maldives, that means it was refueled, which means it had to land. I believe it also means that its purpose or mission lies somewhere far to the west of anywhere that anyone is looking—Africa."

"Lot of assumptions there, Jack. Keep talking."

Jack felt himself growing agitated as his vision came together. "Imagine for a moment. Look at this map. What is the number one hate target of these freaks, other than the United States?" He pointed on the map.

"Israel," said Minchao.

"Right. So plot backwards from Israel. It's about an hour's flight time from somewhere in Sudan—or pick the Central African Republic (C.A.R.), or the Democratic Republic of Congo (D.R.C.), or for that matter Somalia. Those are some of the most violent, lawless places on earth. If you could get a 777 into Sudan, let's say, and hide it effectively for a few weeks or months—at leisure—until you were ready to attack, all you'd need is sufficient fuel, and a few mechanics to make sure everything on board is functioning."

"So where would you refuel this plane?"

Jack pointed again on the map.

"Bay of Bengal," Minchao said.

"Right. Think about it. If you know what you are doing—which these people clearly do, and they have bided their time for over a decade to pull off a stunt like this—you will figure out each of the smallest details. You might for example remove the emergency signaling devices and fly them south off the coast of Australia to make everyone search high and low, when in reality the plane never went south at all. Instead, you fly into the Bay of Bengal, land at a carefully chosen location, and refit for the flight to Africa."

"You mean refuel?"

"Yes. You're only fueled for Beijing—can't reach Africa."

"What about the people on board?"

"They will all be dead by now. Your landing is for multiple reasons. It's a brief but important refit."

Minchao made a horrified face. Jack had already passed his personal point of horror. "There is a reason why the plane was flying low when the fisherman saw it over the Maldives."

"Avoiding radar?"

"No. Its doors were blown. It was depressurized."

"Explain."

"We know the plane reached its cruising altitude at 35,000 feet. Suddenly, at the point just before it made that westward turn over the Gulf of Thailand, everything changed. Let's assume the terrorists figured out a way to sabotage one door, like planting explosives in the locking mechanism earlier during routine maintenance. If you blew the door out, pressure inside the cabin would almost instantly drop. Worse yet, the temperature would drop far below zero in seconds. The air inside would turn into a dry, whitish haze. The passengers' lungs would freeze. They would die in a few breaths, too late for their oxygen masks to work."

"And the perpetrators?"

"They would come prepared with masks. They would seize the cockpit, and bring the plane down to a low altitude. Within ten or fifteen minutes or so, the air pressure and temperature would again be livable. Now all the good folks on board are dead."

Minchao sat down, wiping his brow with a handkerchief. "Run this by me again slowly, Jack."

"I will," Jack said. "Remember—if it's true, this is just what happened. The worst is yet to come. These guys have spent over a dozen years looking for new ways to exploit the weaknesses of civilization. They may be hate-filled freaks, but they are not stupid. The attacks on 9-11 were gallingly brilliant. We do nothing for our cause by downplaying their sick genius. Think of the coordinated hijackings on September 11, 2001 in the U.S., with the spectacular attacks on the Twin Towers in Manhattan, a near attack on the White House that was averted by passenger mutiny causing the crash in Pennsylvania, and still, one plane did crash into the Pentagon. They coordinated train bombings in Madrid, and bus bombings in London. Whatever they now have planned will trump and out-do everything they have done in the past."

Jack carefully laid out the plot so far, as best he could reconstruct it from very fragile and circumstantial evidence. The enemy were exceedingly good at covering their tracks.

"Let's keep it vague, and just assume they blew a hatch, depressurized the interior, killed everyone, and seized control of the cockpit. Maybe they had prepositioned breathing equipment, just as they prepositioned a wad of Semtex-type plastic explosives inside the door locking mechanism.

"I am going to create an artificial unit of distance measurement here, which does not need to be exact for our purposes. It's just a handy tool for the moment until we are thinking more clearly. Remember, the plane took off from Kuala Lumpur and flew northeast toward Vietnam. About forty minutes into the flight, it was seized by these Al Qaeda types and flown west. An hour later, there is a radar contact with the military base near Penang, whose radars last spot the plane 200 miles northwest of their position, and apparently flying west into the Indian Ocean. What if it was flying due north from there into the Andaman Sea in the Bay of Bengal?"

"Go on."

"The aircraft is designed for maximum flight speed around 580 at high altitude, where the air is thinner. It can comfortably fly at 500 m.p.h., or 800 kilometers per hour.

"From KUL to the turning point, and from there to the Penang region, is about the same flight time and distance, so we are describing a roughly equilateral triangle.

"From there, Flight 777 will run out of fuel in about two hours, so its range, unrefueled, is becoming more limited by the minute. Where do we fly it? Into the Bay of Bengal. Everyone is busy looking for the plane to the south, in the Indian Ocean off Australia.

"In the Bay of Bengal, the world's largest bay, are over 750 islands, most of them uninhabited. They include some of the most remote and hostile places on earth. On at least one of them, there are Stone Age hunter gatherers who violently resist any effort to contact them—the Sentinelese natives. There is another horrifying secret here that I have learned about from doing internet searches. I'll tell you about that in a moment.

"Somewhere in the Bay of Bengal, probably in the Andaman Sea close to the shores of Myanmar—Burma—is an island on which they have prepared a landing strip. The 777 requires a runway of about two miles. In this sort of situation, outside the bounds of safety or reason, any flat, hard surface will do—like a barely submerged coral reef, or a coastal road on which hardly anyone ever travels at night. Remember, you are going to touch down for as short a period as possible. I am going to arbitrarily say you can accomplish your mission within an hour, and be airborne again in the direction of Africa."

Jack was able to present Colonel Minchao with a horrifying scenario—reminding him this was probably what had happened—and did not take into account the spectacular military operation planned by the masterminds of terrorism.

Jack rolled the flight clock back to zero.

5.   Jack's Scenario

Flight Clock 00:00: the plane takes off from KUL 00:41 a.m.

Flight Clock 00:20: the plane reaches 35,000 ft altitude twenty minutes later, at 01:01 a.m. KUL

So far, so good. Now, however, the unknown happens on board.

At Flight Clock 00:40 (01:21 a.m. MYT) hijackers take over the aircraft over the Gulf of Thailand, in the dead spot where Malaysian ATC turns over control to the Vietnamese ATC. This is right after the infamous signoff, *Goodnight Malaysian Flight* [777], two minutes earlier.

Simultaneously, at Flight Clock 00:40, hijackers blow out a window or a door to decompress cabin. Thus, passengers and crew die at 1:21 a.m. MYT.

All contact with the aircraft ceases.

Flight Clock 01:34 was that last primary radar contact by Malaysian military 200 miles (320 km) NW of Penang (opposite of intended direction) 02:15 a.m. KUL. Kuala Lumpur to Penang area should only take about 1 hour. But they took the long way around, since this a distance of about 161.12 miles or 259.31 km. Traveling at 500 mph should be about 30 minutes but took 1 hour. That is because they flew in a triangle: northeast from KUL, then West from halfway between Malaysian/Vietnamese air control space, so the two legs add up to one hour exactly.

From Penang to Andaman region off Burma is (let's say) about five to six hundred miles, so they set down on some Bay of Bengal location (yet to be identified) around one hour after Penang, or about 3:00 a.m. (accounting for climbing & coming down).

We are at Flight Clock 3:00 a.m. by KUL 3:40 a.m. landing on a secret location in Bay of Bengal for refitting. Several things happen now.

One, refueling begins. This can be done, pumping standard Jet-A kerosene fuel from a small tanker. Note that, with the cabin pressure blown, they will not climb back to 35,000 feet and therefore will not need the antifreeze additives used to keep engines from icing at high altitudes. Cheap diesel might do it, with some TLC thrown in to keep the engines from being damaged.

Second, you may decide to paint over the Air Malaysia logos, although you will not have time to obliterate all traces of the carrier's identity.

Three, you want to dispose of 241 bodies and baggage, or about 250 tons of material. Since you have a tanker, you can load the baggage on board and sail away someplace to dispose of the baggage.

What about the bodies? A horrifying scenario presents itself, illustrated by a 1945 event that remains one of the most bizarre episodes in the history of warfare. Remember that the world's largest predatory lizard is the saltwater crocodile. This top of the food chain predator can grow well over twenty feet long. It has no natural enemies in the world. Its range includes northern Australia, the coast lines and rivers of Malaysia, the Philippines, Southeast Asia, and Singapore among others, plus the entire Bay of Bengal.

This brings us to the true story of Ramree, an island off the shore of Myanmar (Burma). This is one candidate for the refitting.

In January 1945, Japanese forces were encircled and defeated on the seaward side of the island. Rather than surrender, the Japanese commander ordered his troops to cross the island during the night. The story illustrates the remote and primeval nature of islands in the Bay of Bengal, for one thing. The island is covered with swamps in which it would be easily to lose an army, especially men struggling in the dark of night with heavy rifles and backpacks. Some of them will become stuck in the mire and drown. The real horror is that for hundreds of them, their path of retreat will create a feeding frenzy for packs of saltwater crocodiles. British forces, who provide the only reliable accounts, tell of hearing screams and gunshots all night. As many as 900 Japanese soldiers may have been devoured by those packs of giant, unstoppable reptiles whose savage appetites are boundless.

In our scenario, the terrorists have about forty troops on the scene. The small fuel tanker will have a barge in tow, without an engine and therefore no way of leaving an oil or gasoline slick when sunk. The forty troops take less than an hour to throw bodies from the fuselage down into the barge, as well as unloading baggage into the tanker itself. There must not be any trace left for searchers to find and deduce the real stratagem of the hijackers. The terrorists finish their actions within an hour. They have one more task to perform. They load piles of desert camouflage netting into the cockpit, and then position themselves inside for the long trip to

Africa. The tanker, having fueled the plane and taken on the baggage, sails away. It tows the barge after it, which it will take to some location like the infamous estuary on Ramree itself. There, the barge is sunk—creating a shark-like feeding frenzy of thrashing, whirling saltwater crocodiles, many of them longer and more massive than horses (although lower to the ground). Nobody will pay much attention to a rusty old barge half sunk in some obscure bay. And there will not be a trace of human remains to be found.

In one hour, the plane is ready to take off. Where does this happen? It is hard to imagine a two mile runway on an island, though possible. Most likely, the terror planners have identified a two mile stretch of road that is largely abandoned at night. They only need it for one hour.

(Flight Clock 4:00) the plane takes off from the Bay of Bengal. It is 4:40 a.m. MYT.

Flies due west for about 1200 miles or let's say 3 hours. To avoid being spotted, must fly in a southerly arc around the base of India and Sri Lanka.

(Flight Clock 7:00) the plane flies over the Maldives Islands, spotted by fishers. The real sighting is near dawn. Then some other folks chime in, but I would ignore them. It is 7:40 a.m. MYT. This is about 300 miles (.66 hr flight) north of Diego Garcia, a complex of islands owned by the United Kingdom, on which the United States leases military bases. From the Maldives, the plane flies another 3 hours due west—roughly 1000 miles.

(Flight Clock 10:00 or MYT 10:40 a.m.) the plane passes 200 miles north of Seychelles toward Somalia coast.

(Flight Clock 12:00) The plane flies another 600 miles (2 hours), crossing the Somali coast at 12:40 pm. MYT.

We assume the destination is not Somalia, which is a violent and lawless region too unpredictable for Al Qaeda planners. Instead, the plane crosses over into Muslim Sudan after another 1000 miles (2 hours) and lands.

(Flight Clock 14:00) lands in Sudan at 02:30 p.m. That is the end of the journey—thus far. Total flight time from KUL to Sudan base: 14 hours. This all happens before the world is any wiser. While the world will spend the next several months fumbling around in the Indian Ocean, the plotters of Flight 777 are busy biding their time waiting for the best moment to fulfill the mission that has become such a stealthy mystery to the world.

6. Move to Diego Garcia

Minchao questioned him: "Jack, what about sightings in the South China Sea of a flaming fireball coming down?"

"Sounds like a pretty routine meteor," Jack said.

"Your ideas are pretty scary," Minchao said. "But possible. What do you think is the intended target in your scenario?"

"That is the most important question now—assuming we agree the plane was hijacked and did not meet with an accident."

"I'll buy into that, Jack. As you say, we can't afford to wait for proof it was not an accident, before we open our minds and consider all the hijack possibilities."

"Okay," Jack said. "Hijacked means there was a purpose, and that means the perpetrators have a plan. From the evidence so far, it is a sophisticated plan, it is working very well—they have the entire world baffled—and we must never under-estimate the enemy." Jack tapped a point on the map with his pen. "The first thing that comes to mind is Israel. Weaponize the plane, and you could take out much of an Israeli city like Haifa."

"People have been talking about a dirty bomb for years. Maybe the moment has come," Minchao said.

"Right, and do we know where all the radioactive waste and the fouled Soviet bomb materials are?"

"I will get word out to my intelligence contacts."

"I hope they have a Plan X, as in X-Ray, because this may be show time for them." Jack added: "During the Yom Kippur War in October 1973, Egypt launched an unmanned aircraft as a drone loaded with explosives that was headed directly toward one of the major coastal cities—Tel Aviv or Haifa. Luckily, an Israeli Defense Forces (IDF) plane happened to be passing by, spotted the rogue plane, and shot it out of the air. The IDF pilot almost killed himself in the process, so strong was the shock wave. There is plenty of precedent in history."

"To reach Israel today, the enemy would probably have to use a shadowing technique," Minchao said.

"You mean have them fly right behind or underneath a regularly scheduled airliner, so that they'd be lost inside the airliner's radar signature."

Minchao leaned over the map, touching it as if his fingertips would pick up the truth. "As an Air Force pilot, I can tell you—the

Israelis helped pioneer the technique of shadowing. When they went long range to bomb the Iraqi atomic reactor at Dimona, their bombers came up behind a regular civilian flight and stayed hard on their tail, so that they would seem like a single blip on radar. The civilian pilots never realized they were being shadowed. Today, I'm afraid, everyone is wise to the technique, and it is a difficult one to pull off. The timing has to be exquisite. Radar is also more sensitive these days. So I would agree—you could hit Israel with less than an hour's flight time—but the Israelis would be ready, don't you think? They'd be looking for jokers to pull a stunt like this."

Jack said: "I agree. I was thinking maybe they could shadow a passenger craft, headed for Amman, Jordan maybe, and peel off at the last minute on a suicide run to take out some juicy target. Something really spectacular. Then I began to have doubts. I started looking for other targets—and other strategies—and wouldn't you know it, I found some that would make your hair curl."

The two men left their conversation off at that point.

Minchao promised to take Jack's proposed scenario up the ladder. What else did they have to go on?

Later in the day, Minchao came back. "Jack, a moment."

"Yes?"

"Diego Garcia."

"Really?"

"Number one, I was able to keep you guys sorted out from the mercenaries, so that's no longer a worry for you on this particular mission. Secondly, I think there is considerable interest up top for your African scenario. We are going to be evacuated to Diego Garcia this evening at 9 p.m., so have your guys ready to go."

For Jack and his Team Gray, Africa would be the next focus of attention. Jack was now the identified architect of an Africa scenario explaining the vanishing of Flight 777. He almost wished he were wrong. The Israel scenario was bad enough, but think of it—Sudan (or C.A.R., or D.R.C., or Somalia) was within reach of the European subcontinent, and of other points representing the world that the terrorists hated beyond any shades of reasoning.

Part Two: Team Gray on Diego Garcia

7.   Arrival on Diego Garcia

The four U.S. military men looked oddly touristy in their casual civilian clothing as they rode on a canvas-topped golf jitney. The ride crossed miles of tarmac at Kuala Lumpur International Airport under partially cloudy, almost drizzly skies. The oven-like tropical day was just about to set in, and Jack felt himself sweating around the collar. Any moment now, the sun would come out and the temperature would climb toward 100F.

Lew Minchao, Ben Latoni, and Ray Marston rode in the jitney with him, driven by a stocky local Filipino man in his fifties. Sitting on the tarmac, fueled and ready to go, was a C-21 like the one that had brought Jack and his team back from the Philippines.

Presently, they were in the air headed west, nursing sodas in the passenger compartment. "So, Jack, you believe in this Bay of Bengal scenario?"

"The more I think of it, yes."

The men frowned, thinking of the horrific implications of the salt water crocodile infestation. Jack had already briefed Ray and Ben on his theory.

Jack told Lew: "I figure about three or four hours into the crocodile swamps, including time to refit and refuel. Add the flight time to the Maldives, and the timing fits very well with the fisherman's report of a sighting."

"And the flight time from Maldives into Africa makes for about fourteen hours' flight total," Minchao speculated. "They could have landed in Africa by evening of the same day they took off from Kuala Lumpur.

Conversation petered out, and the men dozed fitfully in their plush seats as the aircraft—designed to haul flag officers and diplomats—whispered through the stratosphere.

The British Indian Ocean Territory (BIOT) is comprised of the Chagos Archipelago of about 1,000 mostly uninhabited islands—most so tiny that their sum total area amounts to no more than 23 mi sq (60 km sq). The largest of these islands is a coral atoll called Diego Garcia, comprising 17 square miles (44 km sq) of land area. It is a top secret location shared by U.K. and U.S. military forces, said to number about 4,000 permanent cadre at any time.

Diego Garcia, often compared to a stationary U.S. aircraft carrier in the middle of the Indian Ocean, is almost equidistant between Africa and Malaysia. The atoll is roughly 2,000 nautical miles (3,650 km) east of the African coast. It is nearly 1,000 nm (1,790 km) south-southwest of India and Sri Lanka. It is about 2,500 nm (4,720 km) west-northwest of Australia.

The Allies maintain two parallel 12,000-foot-long (3,700 m) runways capable of handling the largest bombers, like the B-52. The island was at one time designated one of the emergency landing spots for the former U.S. space shuttle (along with Easter Island off the coast of Chile, and other spots around the globe).

Diego Garcia is sufficiently remote to offer a safe strategic base of activities, yet centrally located in a large and geo-politically volatile theater of operations. The only fly in the ointment, Jack learned in his research, were some 2,000 natives (Chagossians) who were forcibly relocated when the British acquired the islands in the 1960s. These islanders were sent to start new lives on the Seychelles and Mauritius islands off the African coast, against their will, and were still suing to return to their ancestral home in the 21st Century. It was a high-handed maneuver still barely doable at the height of the Cold War, but something no self-respecting Western power would attempt to pull off in the modern era.

The C-21 carrying Jack and his companions made a smooth touchdown on Diego Garcia's long airstrip toward evening. The command might have many tenant commands and activities, but it was officially a U.S. Naval Support Facility commanded (as a big sign on the landing field said) by one Captain Stuart Antonov, U.S.N., assisted by one Master Chief Petty Officer so-and-so (the top-ranking enlisted person under Antonov).

Jack watched the atoll approaching amid a vast expanse of blue Indian Ocean tinged with the last golden sparkles of evening, and white caps jumping about like bits of sugar frosting.

Diego Garcia is a bit like a necklace open at the top. At no point is its near-circular string of land wider than a mile. Except for the concrete of its runway, air terminal, and U.S. Navy base, it is largely covered with jungle growth topped with palm and other trees. A roadway runs around much of its perimeter—left over from the days when the ground was taken up by plantations that the British bought out in the 1960s as they consolidated power here. Jack had been here before, passing through on at least two past missions, and he always had a mildly unholy, ghostly feeling about the departed native people and the abandoned, overgrown plantations. Aside from fish processing, the plantations had primarily produced coconuts and their byproducts, including meats, cordage, and oils.

In the middle of the casually thrown necklace was a captive lake of water that provided a calm anchorage in all but the stormiest weather. Jack found the most attractive of its several beaches to be Turtle Cove, located at the remotest place inside the enclosed atoll. The cove had pristine sandy beaches framed with high jungle growth, creating an illusion there was more land than there actually was.

The economical structure of the atoll amazed Jack. Had someone designed this place for a purpose, it would be hard to imagine a more efficient way to pack so many features together without crowding—fuel depots, twenty piers and docks, recreational beaches, the airport, administrative buildings—or without destroying the charm of the abandoned plantations and their unpaved dirt roads amid dense forestation overlooking pristine beaches and bays.

Welcoming Jack's team was a female U.S. Navy commander named Mary Rose Rodriguez. She was a tall red-headed woman with dark-green eyes, a mannish oval face, and a no-nonsense attitude offset with an air of quiet self-assurance. Her maiden name, Jack soon learned, was O'Donnell, she was from New Jersey, and there was a Mr. Rodriguez at home, making millions in the U.S.-Costa Rican sugar trade while parenting three school-age children.

"I will be your U.S. liaison for everything you need," Cdr. Rodriguez said as she strode ahead of them across the tarmac. She wore comfortably fitting bluish tropical fatigues, jungle combat boots, and a soft cap under which wisps of golden-red hair caught the glow of a lovely sunset. "Have you eaten?"

"I think we may be starving," Minchao said. "I haven't checked, but my stomach sounds like a propeller plane."

"Good," she said. "We have our own little world here at this facility, staffed by the usual Regional Guest Workers (RGW). Those are third-party nationals, meaning southeast Asians, some Africans, some Sri Lankans, on staff, cooking for us, maintenance, you name it."

"No natives here?" Jack asked.

She shook her head. "The U.S. and U.K. deported all 2,000 native Chagossians or Ilois—Islanders—half a century ago against their will. It's a tragic story, something that wouldn't happen today." She lightened the tone: "There is a British Commonwealth flavor. I hope you like fish and chips with vinegar, because that is the dish they most readily whip together on short notice."

"Can I have mine in newspaper like they do in London?" Ben said. They all laughed, picturing a typical greasy looking cone of newspaper, filled with tidbits.

"I'm afraid not," she said airily. "Newspaper is too expensive to ship here, so we rely on satellite internet feeds in the 21st Century. Economy is the word. Don't worry—you can enjoy sunbathing, swimming, and fishing—if you find time."

They ate together in a rather standard mess hall that you would find at almost any military post in the world. The chefs—a red headed man, a pretty black woman, and an Asian man—were jovial and eager to please. Malay looking maintenance engineers drove about in golf carts, keeping the area immaculately groomed.

Cdr. Rodriguez joined them for an early dinner. Then she walked them a few hundred feet to a U.S. Bachelor Officer Quarters (BOQ) barracks of concrete blocks biliously painted a faintly luminescent baby food pea color. The three story building had an antiseptic, efficient, heartless cleanliness.

Each team member had a small room of his own. They had just time enough to dump their luggage before joining Rodriguez and Minchao for a short hike along an overgrown jungle path leading to a long, low white building with warning signs all around, and lots of electronic dishes and grids over the top and in the woods nearby. "Welcome to your new duty station," Rodriguez said. "I'll be at the main admin offices down by the beach if you need me. Call or visit." She pointed to a nearby rack of bicycles. "We have a bunch of them, rent free, so if you don't feel like walking, that's the nearest thing we have to a taxi service. You pedal yourself. Just be sure and leave the bicycle someplace covered and visible for the next person." With that, she resumed her long strides and soon vanished in the growing darkness.

Jack and the others opened their door to their new headquarters.

"I can't believe it," Lew said as he gazed across the room.

There was yet another table, with maps and other documents unrolled across it.

"It's like they carried our old roost over here from Kuala Lumpur," Ray said. "I can almost see my old coffee cup rings."

"At least they have more monitors," Ben said. He was the most digitally savvy among them. His mouth seemed to water at the sight of a half dozen large computer monitor displays hanging from the ceiling like Big Brother eyes in a horror movie.

"Go on," Jack said, grinning, "embrace them, Ben. Give them a hug."

Ben staggered forward in mock shock, with his arms upraised, hands open, and eyes faking daze. "Come to papa, babies…"

Commander Rodriguez appeared behind them. "You'll have all the computing power you'd ever need, gentlemen." She stood in the doorway, bracing herself with both arms. "There is just one catch."

"No electricity," Ben guessed.

She laughed. "I wish it were that simple."

"Share," Lew Minchao begged.

"We've had hackers try to hit our systems."

"Oh no," Jack said. "NSA out to lunch?"

"Nobody tells me a thing," she said, strolling toward a coffee bar with lanky, easy movements of her long gestalt. "I was told to warn you, that's all."

Ben stretched his arms in both directions. "So what does that mean? We can't type anything important on our screens? What fun is that?"

"Yeah," Ray said, "how's a man supposed to get any meaningful work done?"

"I am going to make a huge pot of coffee," she said. "This monster before me makes thirty cups at a whack. I think we are going to need it."

Ben said: "If we were to be compromised, that means what? The whole network here? Just this room?"

She said: "Good question. The best I can answer is that, for now, we keep all sensitive mission files offline on our local area network. I have guys working on it around the clock, fire walling it and making sure we have all the wagons circled. No pesky pixels get in or out. Meanwhile, the ASCII gods in the atmosphere around us are working night and day to find the rats and snap their necks."

Jack said: "Do we have any idea who these rats might be?"

She finished loading up the coffee maker, which towered like a silver rocket on the counter, and turned. She leaned against the counter and shrugged. "If I know, Captain…"

Ben said: "You have to wonder.…"

"…If it's the same folks who stole the plane," a new voice said.

A look of amusement crossed Rodriguez's face. "Just in time. I'd like you to meet an old friend. One of our visiting, allied intelligence analysists." She raised a hand to introduce him.

In the doorway behind them stood an olive-skinned man wearing a dark-gray jumpsuit without markings on it, and a red and black checked *keffiyeh* pulled down like a scarf under his jacket collar. His black eyes flashed, in contrast with a handsome mouth full of sparkling white teeth under a sharply trimmed little mustache. "At your service," he said through dimples and utter charm. "Dr. Mustafa ibn Malik, diplomate and Ph.D. in Computer Sciences." He bowed slightly from the waist.

Commander Rodriguez completed the introduction as Jack and the men respectfully—and curiously—stepped back to open the way for their guest. "Meet Prince Mustafa, 250th or so in line for the throne of the Kingdom of Saudi Arabia. He is also a black belt in Brazilian Jiu-Jitsu, an award-winning Tango dancer married to a Spanish lady who teaches poetry in Cairo, and a colonel in the Saudi Air Force. Aside from that, he is a member of the U.S. astronaut corps on standby until we get the next generation of orbital bicycles rolling again."

"Wow," Ray said.

"Wow," Ben echoed. "Can he fix a computer though?"

Jack clapped lightly. "Welcome."

Prince Mustafa bowed again. "I am honored. Please, let's forget the formalities. I prefer to go by the name Donald."

"Not Duck," Ray said.

"Quack," Ben said.

"Duck if you must," Donald said, "but I'll stand upright as we make forward progress."

"I want to go home," Ben said.

"I want to stick around to see what happens next," Ray said.

"My companions are comedians," Jack said.

"Call me Don. It's easier on the mustache," the prince said as he stepped around shaking hands.

"Don is a member of our larger crisis group," Rodriguez said. "Tell them."

The Saudi prince assumed a teaching stance, with his hands modestly folded over his belt. He had a tendency to speak in a modulated, formal voice. "The Commander is correct. My government is already convinced that we are in the midst of a serious terrorist plan by extremists who unfortunately and erroneously claim to be of the same faith that I profess—Islam. It bears to remind everyone that the stability of the Middle East is critical to the stability of the world, and thus my government and these perpetrators stand at opposite ends of the spectrum. We may not always agree with your government, but then what relationship is ever completely without arguments? In this matter, our interests coincide. Whatever these terrorists are planning, my government will be in the forefront to stop them." He raised his hands in a gesture of reason. "As you will see in my fellow team leader, who is on her way over, these are times that call for new answers to old questions."

As he spoke, a gray-haired woman appeared in the doorway—stopping to look about the room, inclining her dramatic gray eyes in respectful greeting. "Welcome to Operation Cocos Weather," she said.

"Formerly Operation Missing Airplane or MAP," Jack said. "I can't keep up with the changing names."

"I know, it's a silly name game, but a very serious operation. I don't know if any spies will be thrown off by these names, thinking we may be meteorologists, but your government draws these things out of a hat, so we have no control. It's just as well."

Cdr. Rodriguez made the introduction. "Meet our other Assistant Team Leader, Dr. Rebekah Goldstein, who is a chief executive with an international engineering firm with offices in London and New York City. She is also a reserve IDF colonel based in Tel Aviv, specializing in digital intelligence and satellite interferometry—or so I am told." Rodriguez's modest laugh indicated she did not expect to actually know the full contents of Goldstein's resume. Rebekah Goldstein was a modest seeming women of about fifty, with gray hair, large gray eyes that lingered on what they wanted to absorb. She had that quality, Jack observed, of studying people rather than just looking about. He quickly had the feeling that he and his team had landed among some very capable souls.

"So you see," Rodriguez said, "we have a bit of a United Nations going here. I wanted to introduce you to the two assistant team leaders to give you a feeling for our intel without borders, as one might call it."

"So who is the chief team leader if these two are the assistants?" Ray asked.

Don cut in with his soothing but dominating voice: "You will not be meeting him, since he is apparently based out of London. His name is Metrado, and all we know is that he is a highly placed international figure with lots of contacts. If that sounds vague..."

"...We feel the same way," Rebekah Goldstein said in her barely accented English, "I have not met Metrado, and I think Donald here has only met him once." Her English accent sounded like an intriguing, subtle mix of U.S., British, and modern Hebrew that Jack couldn't quite pinpoint—and accents were one of his minor, useful passions. As if cued by telepathy, seeing the looks around her, she added: "And I grew up in South Africa, in case you wonder about my accent." She added: "Of course, to me you all have accents and mine is the neutral, received English."

They introduced themselves all around, shaking hands, nodding, and smiling. The chemistry in the room was eager and cooperative, very positive.

"We will get you caught up," Don said, folding his hands together as he often did, and pointing with them. "Captain Dorsey, we received your proposals through channels and found your suppositions to be plausible. That is why we asked that your government fly you to our operational headquarters here. You should know that we are monitoring the entire panoply of search, rescue, and recovery operations across the South and Southeast Asian theaters. Your scenario building staff will be a small subset of what we are doing, but we will be watching your results with the utmost interest. Frankly, you have the most enviable and imaginative assignment of all. And—since I understand you are at heart a Special Forces unit—I am sure you will enjoy your time here as a kind of diversion, maybe even a vacation of sorts, since we will not ask you to march across great distances on rough terrain carrying large backpacks." He winked and grinned. The men laughed. "Although the possibility exists that you will be airborne on a moment's notice to a theater of tactical operations the minute we have any solid leads." He added: "Know also that there are other Unconventional Warfare units on standby here, and on mainland locations around us—Africa, Arabia, Israel, India, Thailand, to name just a few—ready to assist."

Rodriguez added: "The U.S. Navy also is flying in a SEALs team from San Diego on stand by, so you won't be alone."

Ben Latoni said: "Cool—we trained with some of those guys, so we may know them."

Jack explained for the benefit of Rebekah, Don, Lew Minchao, and Mary Rose Garcia: "My Army detachment spent some time with the Navy's Special Warfare Command in Coronado, and in turn they trained with us in a Central American jungle location."

"Very efficient," Don said with the air of one who is eager to wrap things up and get back to whatever he was doing before. "We are all cross-trained and without borders. I have high hopes that we'll solve our mystery—what happened to Flight 777."

"Even more scary," Rodriguez said, "what's going to happen next?"

"We'll have to out-think them," Rebekah urged.

With that, the party broke up.

Rebekah and Don returned to their offices in a nearby building, while Jack and his team made themselves familiar with their new digs.

"Just to warn you again," Rodriguez said, "use the Internet as needed to download passive info, but don't cross-chat. Use our back channel intra-mail on the LAN instead. If that is compromised, our local engineers will be able to track the bug or virus down immediately. We have a team scrubbing our local area network with fine-toothed combs. Store all your files locally until we get the all-clear. Above all, don't post any ideas or evidence where a possible hacker can find them."

Jack was to gradually notice, as time went by, a mix of U.S. military, U.S. civilian, and southeast Asian FNE engineers maintaining the hardware and software on the local computer systems. This struck him as a bit odd, and he filed it in deep memory for later reference.

In his work area, that hanging bank of computer screens overlooked a pretty traditional sea of maps still smelling faintly of fresh ink and paper—and a limitless urn of coffee. Jack's team must begin organizing a lot of nothing and chaos into whatever coherent structure of information they could.

"I'll be your liaison with Commander Rodriguez and the world at large," Colonel Lew Minchao told Jack, with a nod to Ben and Ray who listened attentively to his out-briefing. "I'll be like a butterfly, fluttering between your command post here and the offices of Operation Cocos Weather."

Ben said: "I know—we'll call ourselves Operation Coconut."

"Operation Coco-Nuts," Ray said. "Or just plain Nuts. Right, Boss?" He looked at Jack.

Jack replied with a laugh and a wave. Amid camaraderie, traditional lines of military hierarchy were still in place, like a satellite handshake, subtle but solid. This was so ingrained in the psyche of any uniformed person that it bore little verbalization—just an occasional acknowledgement. With the loss of Captain Robert Keaka, Captain Jack Dorsey was the commanding officer of Project Coconut, or whatever the fellows wanted to call it. He would call on Assistant Team Leaders Goldstein and Donald in the morning to establish his credentials and mesh his team's gears with theirs. He was sure there was already a numerical designation, if for nothing else, for payroll purposes, and probably a message traffic code or node. For now, Operation Coconut was good enough. It was simple in concept and scope, and it worked.

Each man on the team need not verbalize the other dynamic going on. Each had his thoughts about a spouse just recently separated by circumstances after a happy vacation—and a comrade and friend, Robert and Marian, now lost and possibly deceased. It gave everyone a sense of purpose, of focus, and determination.

As the tropical days in March and April rolled by, the missing flight mystery deepened. Every promising lead fizzled out. The entire world remained puzzled, despite the most expensive and expansive ocean search in history.

Jack and his companions adapted to a routine. Every morning, they would eat together at the mess hall near the airfield. Then they would spend their days waiting for a call to action. Meanwhile, they pored over their maps, watched news and incoming message traffic, and made sure they stayed fit and ready.

Jack noticed that the uniformed personnel on base seemed to be growing more numerous—something was building. Perhaps a routinely planned exercise was swelling the ranks, or maybe someone higher up had info nobody else yet did. Jack noticed a lot of tropical twill flight suits and a lot of bluish-toned Navy camouflage utility uniforms. Over 2,000 Foreign National Employees (FNE) worked on the island in every imaginable capacity, from maintenance to cargo handling, from the mess halls to the commissaries. Many were Filipino or Filipina, usually friendly and helpful. They had their own little recreation spots to relax and chat in their home tongues. Some of the guest workers seemed to like buying model cars and airplanes at the Base Exchange or BX, and flying them over the beach with remote controls while listening to music and chatting during their off-duty hours. It was a small community, all told, and one formed little relationships here and there. Jack took a liking to a pretty young cash register attendant at the main BX, whose name tag read Nessie Galayan. She wore a wedding ring on her light-skinned hand, and looked a bit more Guamanian than Filipino. She always flashed a big smile when Jack came through her register.

After breakfast, Jack's team would walk to a meeting in the admin building, holding tall paper coffee containers. Amid the routine, they got to know each other better. Commander Mary Rose Rodriguez would always kick these meetings off, standing at a lectern surrounded by men and women in various service and national uniforms. By now, Rodriguez had confided that she was known to her friends as Maro (Marie Rose), pronounced like Sorrow or Tomorrow. She welcomed the Team Gray to call her that informally. With her reddish hair coming loose in wisps, and her competent, friendly facial features and soft eyes, she was becoming a kind of alpha female to the men.

Maro took Jack, Ben Latoni, and Ray Masterson on a tour of the island. She rode shotgun in an ancient Jeep, from pre-Hummvee days, with a blue and white striped canvas awning someone had improvised on the old ragtop frame. The driver was a young yeoman in crisp blue-white Navy utility uniform with combat boots, light-skinned, blue eyed, with honey wisps of hair parted in the middle under her uniform cap. Her name was Jessica Napoleon—tall, lanky, a Samoan-American from Salina, Kansas.

The ride started at the northwestern tip of the roughly horse-shoe shaped land area situated in the middle of the Indian Ocean. As in military facilities everywhere, the U.S. Navy had created a neatly painted, tidy arrangement of buildings and facilities for work, living, and entertainment. There was a coastal road that followed the entire necklace from top to bottom and back to the top again on the other side, broken only by the open bay at the north end. Three islands rose from the water in the bay opening.

Maro explained: "The atoll is about 67 square miles, or 174 kilometers square. The rim is about forty miles along, forming an elongated circular figure broken at the top by a breakwater of sand bars with three islands on it. Inside is a lagoon thirteen miles long north-south and at its widest, seven miles across. As you can imagine, there is wonderful sport sailing and kite boarding on it, in spots where it may be allowed. The opening at the north end is about four miles across. The shelves on all sides drop steeply into deep water."

With fresh wind blowing through his hair and sunglasses, Jack felt relaxed and enjoyed the ride. The other two men smiled amid their thoughts as the Jeep churned along. In the back of the Jeep, Jack sat on the left, Ray Marston on the right, and Ben Latoni on the back of the seat, almost on the rear of the vehicle and hanging on as Jessica Napoleon smartly maneuvered on the roads.

On the ocean horizon were gray Navy ships and tankers, busy at their missions of sustaining U.S. military operations on three continents—Africa to the west, Asia to the north and east, and Australia. The fourth continent, to the south, is Antarctica.

"We are on the intersecting paths of much commercial and military air and sea traffic here," Maro explained. She wore fatigue uniform, like Jessica Napoleon. Maro, being tall, had to sit a bit sideways to fit into the small sea, with one long leg and combat boot on the outer running board of the early 1940s designed vehicle. Maro's red hair was pinned back under her fatigue cap, full and rich, falling in a page boy cut chopped off high over the collar in back where a non-regulation pony tail might have been. In fact, she explained at one point that, like a lot of service women, she had pinned up her hair until she'd grown tired of it in the tropical heat and dampness and whacked it off.

"This is still part of the U.K.'s British Indian Ocean Territories," Maro explained. "We lease Diego Garcia from the U.K. In the 1960s, the arrangement was that they turned Diego Garcia over to us after expelling all the native islanders.

"If you think about the Indian subcontinent, and the large island of Sri Lanka near its southern tip in the Indian Ocean, imagine a long string of atolls, reefs, and a few islands stretching south from there—thousands of these, grouped into archipelagos. A long underwater mountain range runs north-south, called the Chagos-Laccadive. All these little specks of land are mountain tops, including the coral atolls like Diego Garcia that have grown up over millions of years and turned into islands. The sea on either side of us here is quite deep. Maldives is one archipelago just south of Sri Lanka—which is where the fisherman spotted our missing airliner flying low over the ocean, presumably heading west toward Africa.

"South of the Maldives are hundreds more islands and other mostly tiny, uninhabited specks of land in the blue ocean—which is the world's third largest ocean after the Pacific and Atlantic Oceans. This includes the Chagos Archipelago, of which Diego Garcia is the largest and most southerly.

"The Equator passes through an atoll in the Maldives, which is a little over seven degrees of latitude north of here. The Equator crosses through Central Africa, and the Indian Ocean south of Sri Lanka, and across the Asian continent through Indonesia—just south of peninsular Malaysia where the missing aircraft originated.

"So Diego Garcia sits in a kind of imaginary crosshairs, halfway between Africa and southern Asia, and just south of the Equator halfway between India and Antarctica. It's like a U.S. aircraft carrier in the middle of the region, far from land. We support heavy aircraft including C-17s, B-52s, and other huge planes on missions over the Gulf, Afghanistan, and other theaters of operation. We also supply fleet units including carrier battle groups traveling around the world."

The drive took them about an hour around the island, slowing here and there for a look. Almost always, the open ocean was visible on one side, and the large central lagoon or bay on the other side of the narrow strip of land forming the necklace of the atoll. At the south end was Turtle Bay, a picturesque body of greenish-aqua salt water framed by tall jungle growth including palm trees and some tropical hardwoods. There are lots of bird species, plus the island has its share of these wild burros we'll see as we drive along. They are what's left of the old plantations from the 18th and 19th Centuries, which gave the islands some of their export economy. Fishing was the other main livelihood of the islanders."

Jack asked: "So where are the islanders now?"

"It's a sad story," Maro said. "There have been humans here for centuries. It's like the plant life. Seeds drift on the currents and end up here, taking root. I've heard that the vegetation here is forever changing because it is at a crossroads. Same thing with the human population. There may have been some indigenous islanders or Ilois. Over centuries, they were added to by fishing people from around the region, plus escaped slaves of the French, Portuguese, and English. As ships called here—it was even a coaling station for British ships at one time in the late 1800s—they of course brought with them more seeds and bird species. After World War Two, with the Cold War—the Soviet bloc on one side, and the U.S.-led West on the other hand—we had a policy of forcibly evacuating native people from across the Pacific Ocean and the Indian Ocean as if they never existed. In the Pacific, we conducted atomic bomb tests, and moved native cultures off their land by military force—like swatting flies. They never had a chance. Today, nobody would tolerate that kind of high-handed, colonial behavior. Nearly a century ago, that was considered an entirely natural way for white people to treat colored people, to put it bluntly.

"The U.S. and U.K. didn't want the native Chagossians here, for security reasons. So they moved all 2,000 of them west to Mauritius and Seychelles off the coast of Africa. They haven't done very well there, with alcoholism, suicide, and so on. They received very little compensation, and the way they were removed was brutal and abrupt. You'll see shortly how their ghosts linger here."

The Jeep tooled along the coastal road, northward among beautiful, palm-lined beaches on either side. About halfway up the road, they entered an area of dense jungle vegetation. In the growth, Jack glimpsed dimly lit ruins of stone and metal structures.

"Right about in the north-south center of the atoll, opposite the main airfield on the west side, on the east side is this jungle area on the east road. The lagoon tightens a bit in the center. That is where the Chagossians had their main settlement for work and living. There are ruined coconut processing plantations in their, and other structures abandoned long ago. The roads are unpaved, and overgrown in there. Let me show you something."

Jessica Napoleon drove off the main road, onto a side road that quickly descended into thick, shadowy forest. Ghostly remnants of walls, houses, and a village church passed by. At Maro's direction, Jessica pulled over at an overgrown wall of rough stones. The two women and three men climbed out and walked on the shady, relatively cool street. "This is the Ilois or Islander cemetery," Maro said. "Let's be respectful as we take a quick look."

Gingerly, they trod along mossy flagstones into the tight little yard with its sunken tombstones. Many of them were stone crosses, a few of them weeping angels with tears of moss streaming down cherubic cheeks.

It was a haunted, sad place, and a spell of silence descended on Jack's party as they ambled along broken paths. Birds chattered above. Occasionally, wings broke through leafy crowns as a nesting bird went hunting for food. Small animals rooted in holes, while insects carried on their own Diego Garcia in ant hills and other tiny structures.

Jack was glad to stretch his legs, but more glad to get back to the Jeep. "Let's get back in the sunshine," he said.

As the Jeep tooled back to the main road and turned right or north to leave the haunted plantation of long ago, Maro explained: "The Ilois or Chagossians had a life here. The U.S. and U.K. authorities at that time, in the mindset of the times, felt it was best to exercise total control—so they removed the native people, and brought in 2,000 guest workers to handle cargo on the docks, and other functions—maintaining the fuel stores at the tank farm, staffing the mess halls and base exchanges, all kinds of jobs."

"The Chagossians couldn't return to their island?" Ray asked.

Maro shook her head. "When they were removed, it was done by the British, with help from the U.S. military. They gassed all their pets and cut off food shipments to intimidate the islanders, and forced them to leave their furniture and other belongings because the evacuation charters were small ships that could not handle much except the islanders, a suitcase or two, and the clothes on their backs. They are now living in squalor on Mauritius and Seychelles off the coast of Africa, and suing in British and U.S. courts for the right to return."

"You'd think they would make a loyal population here," Ben Latoni said.

Maro shrugged. "Most of us feel sad for them, those of us who care enough to learn their history and understand what was done to them. It was common during the last years of the colonial era. It would probably not happen again today."

"I'm not so sure," Jessica said. "There were rumors that we kept prisoners illegally on Diego Garcia during the 2000s—stories about this being a transit point for black sites, renditions, torture centers for political prisoners."

Maro nudged her, and Jessica fell silent. "We're military and not allowed to speak up about those sorts of stories and rumors. Get you in a lot of trouble, girl."

"Mum's the word," Jessica said, though an angry blush spread over her cheeks. Her lower lip jutted at a stubborn angle. Her small hands gripped wheel and shift stick with extra sharp motions.

Maro said gently: "The Chagos Islanders are negotiating to see if they can at least come back to tend the graves of their ancestors. That's a foot in the door for future progress."

Emerging back in the sunshine on the main road, they welcomed the island breezes and ocean vistas of their magnificent environment. The drive took them to the northeasternmost tip of the necklace, called Barton Point. Alternating with dense jungle were clean work, living, and recreational areas as on any distant military base were junior enlisted folks pulled a one year tour of duty. It was beautiful, remote, and lonely—a nice place to visit, and one to remember fondly upon return to civilization; not a place to linger.

That sentiment, expressed by Jessica Napoleon, and seconded by Ben and Ray, was one that brought Jack's thoughts home to the ranch in Temecula, with its sandy hills and deep palm tree rifts populated by eagles, hawks, mountain lions, and coyotes, not to mention the other desert denizens like scorpion, rattlesnake, and various pleasant species of spiders—all of whom had to make their living, after all, feed their young, maintain a home, and work long hours. Jack thought of his sister Janet, her husband Mark, and above all Catherine and the baby that was due in a few weeks. Making the long drive back to their hangar near the airstrips, Jack and the men thanked Maro and Jessica for the outstanding and informative tour.

Jack's first instinct back in the hangar was to call home. He noticed Ben and Ray doing the same.

Satcom got you linked up over the oceans and halfway around the world. Soon, Jack was speaking with Catherine, who was happy to hear from him, feeling well, and hoping he would be home soon. She knew he was on one of his missions, with no idea what, and knew not to ask questions in that regard.

Over time, Jack also on occasion spoke with Catherine's family in Arizona—who owned an ice cream factory on the outskirts of the hot desert city of Tempe. Catherine had two brothers, both Phoenix businessmen and military veterans, and a sister named Laura who had married a Los Angeles film producer. As with all large families, there was the alcoholic cousin who crashed the party from time to time, as well as a sibling who always married the wrong guy in between divorces, and so forth. Never a dull moment—but Jack and Catherine were considered a newly formed rock on which a family would surely be launched. Jack kept a calendar on his smart phone, on which he tracked the days to Catherine's due date. She'd gone to Balboa Naval Hospital in San Diego with Jack's sister, and the baby was doing fine. The ultrasound was normal, with a healthy squirming little swimmer zipping around among the shoals and atolls of Catherine's internal sea. He was not allowed to tell her where he was or what he was doing, but they could understand each other between the lines of simple, emotional statements. Sometimes they would simply hold their phone to ear, and sing a little mumbled song together, as if they were sitting on the beach together watching a sunset and holding each other at Coronado or Pacific Beach. He could hear the syllables forming in her throat, and her tongue moving, and felt as if he were kissing her. Sometimes they would stop to kiss each other long-distance. The calls were limited, and over all too soon, but they were what kept Jack sane and healthy.

9.   Island Routine

Much as they missed home and their families, Jack and his team stayed motivated by the painful realization that their good friends Robert and Marian Keaka had most likely met with a terrible fate, high above the ocean of the Gulf of Thailand. Robert and Marian, and several hundred human beings like them, whether Chinese or Malaysian or whatever their nationality, had departed Kuala Lumpur with intact lives and hopes, full of love and ambitions. Somewhere over the horizon on that March night, throngs of loved ones had said goodbye or were waiting—many in Beijing, hard-working Chinese family people who were excited to welcome home a spouse—or a father, a mother, a sister, a brother, or a child. When those 241 human beings had vanished in the air, several hundred lives were forever shattered. None of the families would never again be the same. Moreover, there would need to be a gruesome forensics operation for international mortuary teams once the flight and bodies were found.

The unit had a chaplain attached—Lt. Col. Fred Jackson, an Episcopal priest based at a church in Santa Ana, up the coast from San Diego in Orange County. Father Fred was a short, smart, friendly guy with a sarcastic wit and a heart full of empathy. He'd been a U.S. Marine Corps corporal in combat during the Gulf Wars, and had joined the U.S. Army Reserve after his graduation from UCLA and ordination as a priest. He'd spent active time in other combat zone purgatories with bored, scared, homesick, sometimes wounded, and sometimes dying men and women—he was not someone you needed to explain scared shitless to. He was a little guy, with short graying hair, who could comfort a person just by being there. When he held your hand in a moment of total need, you knew he'd been there before and was just leading you along a path he'd already trodden.

Jack had called Father Fred from Kuala Lumpur, and set up a counseling hot line for himself and the other men. They were in touch with Fred once or twice a week at his parish in Santa Ana. Thanks to the wonders of modern technology, they even had a few live satellite uplinks using video phones so they could see each other as they chatted. Father Fred had taken up the point role in working with the Keaka family, and Marian's family the Lams, in Hawai'i and California or Nevada, where family branches had settled in recent generations. Jack and Fred had agreed that, whenever the current mission ended, assuming everyone was going home in one piece, they should make a stop in Hawai'i and visit with Robert and Marian's relatives along the way home to CONUS.

As the days progressed, a certain pattern had established itself as far as the wider world was concerned. Jack and his friends followed satellite news feeds from the BBC, CNN, and other sources and kept up with world news. An endless series of confusing twists and turns followed in the saga. The governments of Malaysia and China attempted to keep a dialog going, but it was hard because grieving families were certain that their government officials were hiding something. Heads must roll, someone must take the heat, and nobody wanted to be the amputee. Day in and day out, statements followed that often contradicted each other. One moment, the suggestion was that wreckage had been found; such hopes were always dashed. An armada of planes and ships from every nation in the region was scouring land and sea, without result. The cycle Jack noticed was that there would be a moment of excitement, followed by an instantaneous let-down. A plane from Japan, a ship from China, a patrol from Australia—whatever, whoever—would spot some floating pallets, or sheets of riveted metal attached to buoyant material, and there would be a few hours of hope. Hope was always just as quickly dashed, when the discovery turned out to be a lost fishing net, a cargo pod fallen off a long-gone container vessel, or simply a mass of plastic and wooden waste going around and around in a garbage gyre.

To make matters worse, a Force 5 cyclone tore through the southern Indian Ocean off the coast of Australia for several days early in the search, making it realistically all the less probable that a lost air liner, should it have ditched when out of fuel, could have left any survivors on the surface.

The mystery deepened day by day—so the press said—and made the mission of Operation Coconut on Diego Garcia all the more compelling.

Father Fred was in regular touch with the two teenage children of Robert and Marian Keaka attending high school in Honolulu.

Ray Marston's wife Latrice was safely at home with their two teenage boys in St. Louis, Missouri, where it was raining a lot.

Ben Latoni's wife Shelley was home with their small children—a boy aged six, and two girls aged seven and nine—in

Poughkeepsie, New York, which was being inundated by a massive snow storm that kept everyone busy.

As Team Gray commander, Jack attended a commanders' meeting every morning at ten as well. Attending were Jack, Maro (Cdr. Rodriguez), and some newcomers—a SEAL officer fresh in from Coronado, a U.S. Army major, a U.S. Marine Corps colonel, and others; several field grade officers filling one-star flag officer slots on sea and air logistics commands attended with their staffs. In addition to that core dozen, Jack often noticed some military looking civilian types, replete with 200-pushup arm muscles, a few tattoos, and *top secret* sewn across their narrowed eyes—hard to tell if they were CIA, Office of Naval Intelligence (ONI), or other alphabet soup. A number of the attendees had accents, and a few wore Allied uniforms, so there was a growing global interest in the case of the missing airliner.

"We aren't entirely stupid," Jack said one day as he and Maro strolled back to Operation Coconut's lair in the blockhouse near the airstrip after one of these meetings.

"No," she said, "give us a little credit. Obviously, when a functioning civilian air traffic network is compromised—and with it, a lot of military nodes—the governments will take notice. So far, your scenario is probably the most provocative yet."

"Thanks," Jack said as they strolled along a concrete path among tall palm trees, with a humid tropical breeze blowing low tide smells past them. Aircraft came and went in a steady stream here, day and night. The airfield itself really did somewhat resemble two aircraft carriers tethered side by side, with fixed and rotary wing traffic steadily moving in organized chaos over its concrete aprons. "The catch is—."

"We haven't shared your scenario with anyone outside a few close allies."

"That doesn't surprise me," Jack said. "Do me a favor. Don't tell anyone I thought of it."

"Mum's the word, bub."

"Thank you. If I'm wrong, I don't want a lynch mob of angry politicians and generals chasing me into the water."

"Worse yet if you're right, Jack."

"Yeah, I didn't even think of that."

"Think of it this way. No matter what the outcome, heads will roll. Important people will resign. Or they will make less important persons take the hit and resign."

"I'm so glad you handle the political stuff."

"It's my job."

"Are you going to run for office some day?"

"You mean as a civilian? I doubt it. Working with all these visiting Congress people and generals and admirals makes me want to take a long rest. All the politicking is very tiresome. Imagine if we allowed news media in here."

"Your next assignment," Jack said. He resisted the urge to elbow her gently in the ribs. If she'd been a guy—oh well. "You're up for a star some time soon?"

"In the Navy, our next step up the ladder is Captain." She looked at him with that competent, fearless gaze. "I'm on the list, in case that's your next question." Being a captain in the Army, Air Force, or Marine Corps was not nearly as high as the rank of Captain in the Navy or Coast Guard. Colonel Lew Minchao was the equivalent of a Navy Captain; and in both services, the next step was flag officer—meaning a one-star admiral or general. She added: "Do you ever regret going Reserve?"

He shook his head. "I had my stint on Active status. I would never want to make a career of it. To tell you the truth, I'm not sure I want to get into field grade. I like boots on the ground operations."

She laughed. "You're too smart for your own good. Here you are, dreaming up scenarios that have the whole world all shook up."

"I'm just good at connecting dots."

"Better than most people," she said.

"Give me just a few dots and I can draw you a picture."

"Maldives is a single data point," she said. "That's not dots."

"I know, but think about everything that must fall into place for that one data point to be valid. The fisherman was either lying, or hallucinating, or he really did see a white Air Malaysia 777 flying too low over the water, complete with red fleet markings and a Malaysian flag. It struck me as too specific to be someone's vague lie. And of course we know everything about him, to be sure he's not a setup."

"Very impressive."

What he did not share with her was the fact that he had already been vetted for either the Foreign Service or the CIA, but his heart lay in the civilian sector. Still, there was a certain pull about this global concern. "I am actually working on my Ph.D. in History," he said.

"Wow. I'm just an MBA," she said. "You outrank me there." She outranked him in terms of military grades. "What are you going to do?"

"I've thought about teaching at least part time. I'm ABD." That means he had All But his Dissertation in the bag, on a path that had been Magna Cum Laude all the way."

"What is your area of specialization?"

"Classical Rome—specifically, ancient Roman topology and topography."

She giggled a bit. "What does that even mean?"

"Well, theoretically, I can tell you what temple stood where, what road crossed which, and whose house was in what part of downtown Rome back in the days of Julius Caesar or Vespasian or Constantine."

"I'm sure it is endlessly fascinating." She did not sound entirely convinced.

"I find it so—especially when we learn the lessons of yesterday all over again today." To him, History was one of those rare fields that lent themselves perfectly to global operations of whatever imperial power happened to be in alpha position—which, at the moment, was the United States. Any time, any where, it was Zulu Time—the global clock of history's most powerful military and intelligence machine was at work. At one time, the clock of empire had been British—nautical time, or Greenwich Mean Time (GMT), centered outside London. Now the global clock of empire was the Master Clock at the U.S. Naval Observatory in Washington, D. C. This governed Universal Standard Time (UTC), whose nautical GMT referent was the letter Z at zero hours(military alphabet name Zulu). Zulu Time was the index time of operations at any time, anywhere in the world.

Jack felt a pull to duty in the mystique of his country's endless supply lines and operational nodes in a world-wide network of economic and political muscle carried on the sinews of ships, planes, and rubber soles. Others seemed to feel the same way.

Joining them on most walks was Colonel Lew Minchao, who took direction from higher up the food chain to rain orders and gifts upon Team Gray (Operation Coconut, as Ben had dubbed it). Minchao told Jack, with Maro present: "The powers on high will be sending us more team members soon. They are taking your ideas ever more seriously—because they have nothing else to go on, and I think your scenario makes sense."

"It's not about the journey," Jack said, "but the destination. I don't want to think how they murdered those people, nor do I care how they fly bread to the commune." That was a reference to a snide remark once made by G. K. Chesterton about the unrealistic plans of utopian communities. Planners had spent countless hours obsessing on whether bread would be brought to idealized communities by airship or by tunnel, with nary a thought as to who would pay for it or how it would be produced. "What I care about is the destination. Who gets there, and how, and what they do there."

"Well," Minchao said, "to pick up your metaphor, we know what they do there is create more murder and mayhem. Who is probably the same bastards who keep sending shoe bombers, underwear bombers, and knifemen to stab an innocent young trooper to death in broad daylight on a London street." He was referring to the murder of 25 year old U.K. Army drummer Lee Rigby by two Muslim extremists on 22 May 2013, using knives and cleavers after running him down with a car, and then declaring their madness brazenly to police and passers-by. Each of the assailants had received a prison term of many decades.

"What I mean," Jack said, "we know they have done something terrible to the missing air liner. What we now need to do is avert the catastrophe they are planning."

"You can bet that will be something spectacular," Maro said. "They will want to avenge the killing of Osama bin Laden by U.S. Navy SEALS in Pakistan back in 2011. They will also want to outdo what they accomplished on 11 September 2001. So they are overdue for a spectacular action."

"Yes," Minchao said, "and there's the reason we don't share this intel with a lot of people. There's a lot of reason to suspect Pakistani ISI intelligence knew where bin Laden was when we invaded their territory and took him out. You don't know whom to trust around here."

"You do know whom not to trust," Maro said.

Minchao said: "Jack, start picking up the pace. Have your team ready to move if we figure out where to move you to. It's looking a lot like Africa these days, so we'll have you inoculated and briefed on local diseases and what not."

Maro said somewhat possessively: "But Jack will also be working with my contingency teams on some specific scenarios, so you don't own him exclusively."

"I need half your time," Minchao bargained with both.

"We'll see," she said.

"It feels good to be wanted," Jack said. "What are these contingency teams?" he asked Maro.

"It's all your fault," she said. "You have some regional powers quite interested in your ideas."

"People we trust?" Minchao asked as they came to the block house. They stopped a moment, three people outlined against the hazy sea horizon, with wind blowing their hair and rifling their uniforms. In the background, ships passed over water, and aircraft moved in the sky, in a languorous ballet of power—a chess game of logistics and positioning.

Maro said: "The people we trust are the ones who depend on us the most for help and cooperation. They have the most to lose, and the least margins of error."

"You mean the Saudis and the Israelis."

"Those are just two—yes."

"I can think of all Europe," Jack added.

"Right on point," Maro agreed.

Minchao nodded. "Don't forget—the United States still invests more in its military than the entire rest of the world combined. That includes the Chinese, the Russians, all of Europe, you name it. That's why the Brits are happy to lease us their base here on Diego Garcia. We gave them a good deal on Polaris missiles back in the day if they'd get rid of those pesky Chagossians and their pets."

10.   Scenario #1—Israel, with IDF's Rebekah Goldstein

Maro's prediction was to come true soon enough. One day, as Jack and his men laid out field gear on the spacious tiled floor of their makeshift hangar-office, there was a knock on the door.

"May I come in?" It was Rebekah Goldstein, the Israeli intelligence official. A woman of about fifty, she could have passed as anyone's mother on a crowded street. She dressed attractively but demurely in what some would call age-appropriate clothing, which consisted typically of black or dark blue dresses, sensible shoes, nylons, and blouses with little vests and a few modest baubles—an ivory brooch, a gold wedding band that had the same comfortable, worn look as her capable fingers in small, firm hands. She wore clear nail polish, and minimal facial makeup—just enough to liven up a natural pallor and uncommonly sad eyes. But her eyes were her most salient feature—they were slow to look, long to linger, and thoughtful. Jack found that her gaze burned into one. He did not ask about the nature of that faint melancholy that lingered about her. And she was smart. Ph.D. in Economics from London, Colonel in the IDF, expert on aviation commerce and technologies, and workmanly fluent in six or more languages.

"By all means," Jack said. "Please." The men rose.

She entered, carrying a black purse against her hip. "No special courtesies, please. I want to be a member of the team if you will let me."

"We will be honored," Ray said.

Ben offered her a chair, making her smile at the hopeful awkwardness.

"I can stand quite well, thank you. What are you gentlemen cooking up in here?"

Ben and Ray looked to Jack. Ben said: "Where do you want to start?"

Jack said to her: "You tell me. Where do you want to start?"

"Can we talk privately?"

"Of course."

Jack and Rebekah walked outside, where the sea breeze blew as always. A gentle wind ruffled her graying hair as it fluttered above a still youthful and wrinkle-free forehead. "Captain, I understand you identified a threat to my country in your scenario building."

"Yes. Actually, the minute I figured they took the aircraft to Africa, it was kind of a no-brainer to think that Israel would be their most likely target."

"Or a diversion."

Jack had thought about that. "I have been doing a lot of speculation. I am a scholar, like yourself. I don't like to dabble in guesswork much."

"Though it can be fun," she said, with a sudden outburst, a girlish giggle. She never lost that serious inner shadow, not for a second. But the purse of her lightly rouged lips told him she knew how to enjoy life as well.

"We all like to climb in the sandbox now and then," he agreed, feeling sunny about it inside. "I don't allow myself too much leeway."

"Your proposal is sound," she said. "The terrorists fly the aircraft to a predetermined location in Africa. They hide it at a location that will either be at the end of a two mile runway or a road surface, or close to it. Which means it will look like a straight line from an orbital satellite. Israeli air defense has already been coordinating searches with the U.S. Air Force and other agencies."

"Have you found anything?"

"We have candidates," she said mysteriously. She added somewhat deflatedly: "But nothing really strong yet."

"My own superiors haven't clued me in on this."

"Well, dear, I am cluing you in for them. Colonel Minchao and I had this conversation along with Commander Maro just this morning."

"Good. Then we are all singing from the same sheet of music."

"Not an original metaphor, but I like it."

"Countries?"

"Candidates," she echoed. "Well, much of central Africa is in an uproar. Good question. Come, let's walk on this nice path by the water. The air is refreshing, and if anyone is eavesdropping, they will have a harder time of it."

"We are lucky," Jack said.

"Why is that, Captain?"

"Call me Jack, please."

"Of course."

"My team and I are on that kind of basis."

"Please call me Rebekah then. I like that basis."

"So what candidates are you looking at from orbit, looking for two mile runways and what now?"

"Well, Jack, I'm sure you have been briefed since you arrived here. The worst of the worst is the Horn of Africa itself, meaning Puntland and the Somalia coastal strip, which are hardly even countries. They are still utterly lawless. Let's call that Zone A. Then we have the next zone—Zone B—almost as bad, but patchy. That includes Sudan, South Sudan, Central African Republic, and Democratic Republic of Congo. Those are some of the most glaring spots—meaning, if you were an Al Qaeda planner, you'd think about picking a place there to mount the next phase of your 777 operation."

"For how long?"

"We have no idea. We think it's a sliding scale between not long enough and too long. Meaning: they would want to wait a few weeks or months for all the excitement to die down before they strike. On the other hand, no matter where they park the plane, it is only a matter of time before someone sees them, word gets out, and they lose the all-important element of surprise."

"I was wondering about that," Jack said. "It's still a mystery, isn't it?"

"Their strategy is an enigma," she said with a close little smile. "That's part of their operational cachet. They are the hidden ones, like the Assassins of old. They see themselves as powerless, even with support from various sympathizers and governments. Think of how many rogue governments operate in this part of the world. What side would a Moamar Ghadafi or a Saddam Hussein be on?"

"Obviously not with the Muslim extremists," Jack said.

"Quite correct," she said. "The enemy of my enemy is my friend. Your country supplied weapons to Saddam as he attacked Iran in the 1980s. He was your friend because Saddam was the enemy of your enemy. When he lost his war, he went for oil in Kuwait, and suddenly he was your enemy. Saddam was an enemy of Israel, but he was always looking out for himself when he wasn't taking insane risks. He was really nothing more than a very clever, cheap, murderous thug. It would have been best to leave him standing a while, because he was one of the top ten on bin Laden's hate list. Too late for all that now. It's a chess game, and we can waste hours talking about it. Getting to the point, we think that this particular operation has a kind of refrigerator life of no more than six months if that. Meaning, either they fulfill their strategy, or they lose the edge and it fizzles out for them." She regarded him suddenly, sharply. "Have you thought of any other scenarios?"

"A few," Jack admitted. "Honestly, Israel still tops the list for me."

She walked thoughtfully beside him for a few minutes. "Jack, you know that we pioneered the use of shadowing civilian airliners with our military craft on long bombing runs."

"Yes."

"And we were nearly hit by an Egyptian drone airplane full of explosives during the Six Day War."

"Yes."

"And our air space is about the size of San Diego County, if that. So we have to keep an operational umbrella all around us, extending out for hundreds of miles. If someone were to hit us with a weaponized airliner, we would see them coming from far away. We have a very effective air defense system. So I don't think we are your candidate. We remain ever vigilant, but that's my opinion in this case."

"You think it's someone else they are going to hit?"

She nodded. "We will help in any way we can, giving you any relevant intel. There is one thing I would like to remind you of."

"Yes?"

"According to your source in the Maldives, they flew the plane to Africa at a low altitude."

"Yes. They had blown one of the passenger ports to depressurize the interior and kill everyone. They were on the ground no more than an hour in the Bay of Bengal, just long enough to refit, refuel, and take off again. They didn't have time to repair the blown door."

She said: "Yes, and consider also that you can fly a turbojet at a low altitude with fairly common diesel type fuel. If you take it up to altitudes where you need to pressurize the cabin, it also means that the fuel lines on the interior can be affected by icing, and you need special Jet-A or better fuel with antifreeze in it. They probably didn't have that either when they stopped in the Bay of Bengal."

Jack stopped and regarded her. She stopped as well, and said: "I would suspect they will repair that door."

"You think they'll get a replacement?"

She shook her head. "Probably not. They will never again fly passengers on that craft. They will load it with explosives—or radioactive material—or some sort of pestilence vector—and simply seal it up."

"Too bad."

"I know," she said. "Too bad. It would be an interesting exercise to trace the supply lines for 777 door replacements around the world. I think it has to be done."

"I'm sure the FBI or someone is doing it. I hope so."

"I hope so too, but it will be a waste of time. Far better to coordinate with the Russians and Ukrainians to make sure there is no stray radioactive nuclear material on the market for terrorists to buy."

"With Eastern Europe in an upheaval, that won't be so easy."

"No," she said, "but I think the damage has been done. The old Soviet bomb materials have deteriorated by now. If someone carried a suitcase full of radium, you'd see them coming for miles. There would be leakage. Still, you can make a dirty bomb. It can be done. That is what I would spend my time on."

They stood regarding each other for a minute. Jack sensed that the meeting was over. "Will you stay around for a while?"

"Of course," she said emphatically. "I still have work to do here. My country's interest is to make sure the Middle East is as stable as it can be made—not always the most stable, but the less volatile, the better. Talk to my friend Mustafa."

"Donald," Jack said.

She laughed. "Donald. He loves to play at being Western, when he is not racing camels in the desert or shooting his gun off in the dunes of the Empty Quarter. He's a polo champion as well."

Jack and Rebekah walked back to the blockhouse together.

After she left, he briefed Ben and Ray. Newcomers were just arriving in a bus. Team Gray, or Project Coco Nuts, was picking up staff. Jack already knew many of the men—they'd served together in the recent combat theater. It was a small world.

Prince Mustafa ibn Malik, or Donald, appeared at the hangar that afternoon. "Captain Jack Dorsey," he said in that Sinatra-like tone, smooth as cream. "Rebekah has briefed me on your conversation."

"We had a good talk," Jack agreed as he and Don took it outside. This time they sat at a small break area overlooking the bay. It was a circle of concrete benches, each with its own round concrete table, all painted Navy gray and of course with part numbers painted on them.

Don wore an expensive cream-colored linen suit, a white silk shirt open at the collar (with his *keffiyeh* loosely draped around his neck). He wore black Italian leather shoes with punch-patterned, sharp points. He carried a pair of sunglasses, tilted up to rest on short, glossy, wavy hair above a handsome, sharp-featured face with dark eyes, strong eyebrows, a small, raked nose, and that pencil mustache over a spare mouth. His complexion was naturally caramel, and his features showed a faintly African mix of heritages, common on the bridge between Africa and Southwestern Asia.

"You discussed the Israeli option with her," Don said. "I would like to kick around with you another option: oil."

"We're talking potential targets."

"Yes. There are lots of them. Saddam showed that they can take a heavy hit without immobilizing world markets."

Jack could recall news coverage of Saddam's retreat from Kuwait, when he had set all the oil fields in that area on fire. For hundreds of miles, the air had been full of black smoke—plumes of it, long and deadly, rising from exploded wells in the sand and stone around the tiny Emirate. The fires wantonly and peevishly set by Saddam could be seen from orbit by a space shuttle.

"Today's world is a little bit different," Don said. "In some ways, nothing has changed. The established kingdoms and emirates continue to maintain their positions on the world stage. I could speak a bit vaguely and diplomatically here, but it is important we get to the point. The Arab and Muslim worlds have their lines of pressure, their fault lines. We have internal enemies. Bin Laden was a Saudi of Yemeni heritage, whose family became billionaires within the Saudi economic sphere."

"Tough balancing act," Jack said.

"Yes. The House of Saud considered his father a friend. His family of course disavowed him, and he disavowed his Wahhabi upbringing—which is conservative enough—in favor of an even more fundamental, strict Sharia law like that observed by his Taliban allies in Afghanistan. He is dead and gone, but his spirit lives on in what our enemies will strive to accomplish with this stolen 777. Consider it a continuation of bin Laden's strategies, but also consider it revenge for his killing by SEAL Team Six at Abbottabad, Pakistan in May 2011. Remember: right now is the third anniversary of bin Laden's death. Memories are long here in this region. Revenge will wait until its proper time. Passions may cool, but planning is long and deliberate. So be warned."

"I am warned," Jack said, thinking of Robert and Marian. "My men and I lost a fellow soldier and his wife on this plane. It is personal for us."

"I believe you, Jack. It is good that you have your heart in this."

"What are your thoughts then?"

"My thoughts are…" he trailed off, fingering a *misbaha*, or short string of 33 beautiful amber prayer beads whose primary purpose was to count the 99 names of Allah, but which many Arabs thoughtfully finger in a more absent manner. "Nothing remains the same forever. We can be philosophical…but let us speak pragmatically. The world is still dependent on oil. That helps my family remain in power, and stabilizes the world as we see it in our region. Fundamentally, anything that upsets this balance is a threat to the well-being of our royal family and the kingdom. So the question is: how could these renegades hurt us the most?"

"Something to do with oil," Jack said.

"Precisely." Donald fingered his beads, sitting with one leg drawn up under the other on the concrete bench near Jack's bench. "During Saddam's attack on Iran, the Western nations' greatest fear was that someone would bomb the Strait of Hormuz and cut off the supply of oil to the West. Over a third of the world's petroleum is obtained by the Persian Gulf nations, which include Saudi Arabia, Iran, and the United Arab Emirates. Maybe as much as 40% of the world's oil trade moves through this narrow choke point, these straits, connecting the Persian Gulf with the Indian Ocean. The fear all through the early Gulf Wars was that someone—whether Iran, trying to hurt Iraq; or Iraq, trying to hurt the Saudis; pick your combination—would sink one or more of the endless chain of tanker ships moving through this narrow neck of water."

"I understand," Jack said. "Even a rumor of war would cause world spot oil markets to freeze up."

"Think of the economic impact if the Strait were blocked for months. The price of crude would shoot sky-high to hundreds of petro-dollars per barrel. In the United States alone, gasoline would become impossibly expensive. Not only that, but your cities rely on tens of thousands of miles of highways and railroads, particularly diesel-driven stock like trucks and locomotives. In a worst case scenario, food would stop moving to supermarkets. Gasoline would stop moving to your corner gas stations. Factories would close. Farms would run out of fuel. People would start lacking food and other commodities. Need I go on?"

Jack shook his head. "I am starting to think that the practical value of a target in the Strait of Hormuz would exceed the propaganda value of a major strike on Haifa or Tel Aviv."

"Precisely." Donald calmly continued fingering his beads. "In the short term, as allies together opposing the Shi'a regime in Tehran, we in the West have been building pipelines to carry oil overland though the Saudi Kingdom to ports not susceptible to actions in the Strait of Hormuz. Then again, pipelines can be bombed, and the Strait are still a serious choke point. So yes, an attack on Hormuz would be a serious blow to the world economy."

Don pulled a folded sheet of paper from his inner suit pocket and spread it open on the concrete table before them. It was a map of Hormuz, with Arabic and French labels. "You see that the strait is less than forty miles across at its narrowest where that spear-tip of Oman sticks out in the direction of the Iranian naval base of Bandar e Abbas on the north side. There are two narrow shipping channels designed to let deep-draft supertankers through. One channel is designated for entry into the Gulf, and the other for exit. The fear during wars has been of an air strike that would sink one or more freighters, blocking the channels. Under wartime conditions, it would be difficult to say how long it would take to remove the blockage. Not only that, but if Iran were to block the Strait, as they have often threatened to do, it would require at a minimum a ground invasion of that part of Iran, Hormozgan Province, probably with a million troops involved since the Iranians would then put all of their assets into play, including large armies. Half of the water is less than 25 meters deep or 75 feet, and most of it is not navigable by ships with a fully loaded draft of 25 meters. Not only that, but you have a factor called squat that causes a ship to ride even lower in the water as it moves, sort of an underwater dynamic principle, caused by lower pressure along the keel area."

"As well as center of gravity and stability factors," Jack said.

"You have done a bit of research," Don observed.

"A little bit. It's not my area of expertise."

"Imagine a wartime air attack on Hormuz," Don said. "Taking out one or more tankers would cause a smoky, dirty fire that could burn for weeks. Not only that, but other tankers would be stuck in the channel, unable to move forward or backward. If they were to fly a weaponized 777 in at just the right moment, they could cause much havoc."

The two men paused and regarded each other. It was a moment similar to the conclusion of his meeting with Rebekah.

"What do you think?" Jack said.

"We are on heightened alert. The kingdoms and emirates have planned for this eventuality for decades, so we have air defenses and other tactical systems in place. Our troops are well trained to deal with such eventualities. Not only that, but the United States and other Western naval powers regularly patrol the straits just inviting trouble."

"Triggers," Jack said, thinking of U.S. brigades in West Berlin during the Cold War. A Soviet or East German attack on even a small U.S. unit was advertised ahead of time by the United States as an attack on NATO and the USA itself. It seemed to have worked as a deterrent.

"You remember the incident of Iran Air Flight 665 back in 1988, which I just had occasion to look up on line to refresh my memory. This was an Iranian AirBus with 290 passengers on board, which strayed into the path of a U. S. Navy guided missile cruiser, *U.S.S. Vincennes*. Defensive systems on the U.S. ship automatically fired several RIM-66 medium range surface to air missiles. They hit the aircraft, killing everyone on board. These systems shoot first and ask questions later."

"Add Phalanx today," Jack said.

"Yes, Phalanx." He seemed to quote from a memorized user manual: "...A radome-guided M-61 Vulcan Gatling gun with six barrels, capable of shooting 4,500 rounds a minute."

"I've seen them in training," Jack said. "The gun itself is based on Vietnam era technology. It spews out high velocity 22 millimeter projectiles at such a ferocious rate that they can shred any target—probably even a jet airliner."

"I am not sure that Hormuz would be the ideal target for your 777." Don shrugged. "I don't know what would happen if they could get their hands on a small atomic bomb."

Jack shook his head. "I think our intelligence people have made sure that even the North Koreans or ISI can't traffic in small nukes. If they had that, they'd be better shooting it in on a SCUD or other missile."

Don said: "These guys are in for a show. They want to kill a lot of people in a messy way—preferably another target like New York City or the Pentagon. Think of the legend they have to live up to. How do you out-do yourself once you have perpetrated 9-11?"

"I don't envy them," Jack said bitingly.

"The Iranians follow strange politics," Don said, "but I don't believe the mullahs are suicidal. I think you are looking for a Taliban-style terrorist group like Al Qaeda was under bin Laden back at the turn of the century."

"What does that mean in terms of targets then?"

"From Africa?" Don asked.

"Unless they move the plane again."

"As Rebekah tells us, they are running out of time. They have to act soon. Their refrigerator time is getting stale, as she likes to put it. That leaves us with targets in Europe, my friend."

"Ouch."

"Yes. Rome, Paris, London; a sacrilege to mention, but I must."

"You mean—like Saint Peter's Basilica?"

He nodded. "Or the Eiffel Tower in Paris. Or Saint Paul's Cathedral in London. Europe offers a rich mix of targets."

Jack calculated quickly. "I was thinking they could hit Israel with half an hour's flight time. Hormuz would still be an hour or less. And of course Rome is probably three hours' flying time for a 777 at cruising speed."

"You should start talking with NATO staff officers. You'll find a few of them here on Diego Garcia already to talk about other issues in the region."

"Thank you." Jack extended a hand, Don shook it, and they parted on a thoughtful, heavy note. Neither Israel nor Hormuz was ruled out—but other vistas opened up. The possibilities grew ever wider and more frightening.

As Jack walked back alone to the blockhouse, he spotted Maro. She stood outside the hangar door, waving—tall, lanky, and oddly urgent in her body language. He picked up to a jog and arrived by her side a minute later. "Yeah, what's up?"

"Get ready, Jack. Your team is shipping out for Africa."

"Really." He stopped and put a stunned palm to his forehead. For a moment, he felt disjointed. Something fundamental had changed in the atmosphere.

"We have a major lead on the case. Come on, I want you to meet someone."

Amid the urgency and mystery following the disappearance of Flight 777, Jack Dorsey's command post—a work space that was hardly more than a table with maps on it—was filled with more people and new purpose. Team Gray had grown to a dozen Special Forces members from various other units and services. He recognized a few of them with a quick sweep of the eyes—all past team members on Middle East missions, all vetted and battle tested. They squatted or knelt in a semicircle before a trio of officers in U.S. Navy blue camo, in the midst of a briefing in progress, as Jack arrived from a meeting with higher brass.

Maro interrupted a lecture on jet aircraft engines by a Navy pilot to intone: "Meet Captain Jack Dorsey, Acting Commander of Team Gray."

A splattering of applause rippled through the room, along with a few whistles and some *yeah*s and *hooah*s.

Acting? Puzzled but game as ever, Jack followed a flurry of greetings and handshakes to the top person in the center of the room—a young, blond, crew-cut rear admiral, lower half (one star). There followed the kind of instant assessment, by which two leaders read one another in a split second from various markers— from posture, from attitude, from a clinch of the eyes, and from how they shook hands.

Jack noted wing insignia on the man's uniform, and quickly made some guesses. The guy was probably Annapolis, probably a carrier pilot, probably combat experienced, had been to all the major staff schools, and was being groomed on a big time command track. He had sort of a Midwestern Boy Scout look, complete with sharp, handsome features—pale, blue eagle eyes, the whole fearless profile. Sometimes these guys were real, and at other times they were some senior (arguably, by some lights, senile) brass' cardboard imagination of a leader.

Jack walked up, shook hands with RDLM Paul Falk, and knew he was at least dealing with a martial arts champion. As an expert in karate and jiu jitsu, and working on his own martial art variant, Jack had a lot of experience reading handshakes. This man had a grip like a steel claw. You didn't shake his hand—you put yours out there and hoped he didn't tear yours off. The energy of a buzz saw was there, pumping away. That sort of person usually did not work

smoothly with the tea and crumpets set at the admirals' club. Paul
Falk had a little bit something crazy and determined in his laugh,
driven by an obvious refusal to hear no. Surely a military pilot. Jack
liked him immediately. By the time Jack finished shaking hands
with his new boss, and turned to address his team, he felt
comfortable that the Navy had sent the right boss for the job. Falk
had the uncanny ability to immediately sort things out and let a man
know that he was behind him when needed, and before him if
needed, depending on circumstances. It was the kind of instant
oatmeal camaraderie you needed to fly into the face of an
unknowable and horrifying enemy.

"We've heard a lot about you and your team," Falk said in his
unmistakable Maine flat English. If they porked cors in New
Yoahk, and pahked cahs in Bahston, they pehhked cehhs in
Bengehh (Bangor). Falk introduced his own staff. "I have Captain
Shep Sepak of the U.S. Marine Corps on my left."

Jack shook hands with a man whom he assessed as a no-
nonsense, no-advertising, just the-total-goods-and-where-do-you-
want-them sort of Omar Bradley kind of guy. Sadly, he reminded
Jack a bit of Robert Keaka. Gold rimmed glasses gave Captain
Sepak a scholarly look and softened his granite Chesty Puller jaw a
bit. Sepak did have a dry sense of humor. "I understand Team Gray
got its handle because all the other colors were taken."

A laugh rippled around the room, all in good morale.

Falk continued, owning the room with his high energy bursts of
speech. "Let's get to know Team Gray. Or as Sergeant Latoni
informed me when I met the core group earlier, Project Coco Nuts.
That's two words. I'm adding the plural to nuts because of the
added people, not what I think of you guys."

Good humor continued. One by one, the men stood and
introduced themselves briefly. There were seven new additions—
four staff sergeants, two master sergeants, and a first sergeant.

"We are going to function together like one guy with twenty
arms and twenty legs," Falk said in a booming voice. "It's gonna be
that tight and well coordinated. Right?"

Yeah, echoed the room full of mostly male voices. Maro
clapped.

"Most importantly, First Sergeant Boileau, will you please step
up here."

The first sergeant—a master sergeant with a diamond device
between his three chevrons and three rockers—rose and joined Jack

amid popular applause. Every military unit has a commanding officer and a chief enlisted leader. At the company grade, a first sergeant is the top enlisted person. While the officers do officer things, the first sergeant is mother, father, and older sibling to the enlisted personnel. It is an element of military life instantly understood and welcomed as natural by anyone who serves. It is the normal, natural way for things to function according to military tradition. In a special forces unit, the distinctions of rank were usually subordinate to the personal bonding that got men through their ordeal—but still, a first sergeant was as right as rain. His or her equivalent at higher echelons was the sergeant major or command sergeant major. The unspoken expectation was that Project Coconut would not rise to battalion level any time soon— but Jack knew that could change any moment as well. They'd either promote Boileau or bring in a command sergeant major. That, however, was then and maybe—this was now and real, which was all that counted. Falk made the introduction. "Meet First Sergeant Greg Boileau. Where are you from, Top?"

"Las Vegas, Nevada, Sir." Boileau was a short, chunky fireplug of a man with red face, a grizzled crew cut, and flinty black eyes. By contrast, he had a kindly smile and, as Jack found out, another vise grip handshake. It felt like a good team—much needed.

"Did you bring us some Las Vegas luck, Top?"

Laughter rippled through the room as the man sat lounging amid their gear. They never went far from their weapons, which were pyramided in the center with several men guarding them for life's sake. From here on, each man would pick up his choice of weapons and never again part with them.

"I'm afraid I don't gamble, Sir. Mormon, part Navajo, part French."

"What a combination," Falk said. "How very U.S.A."

"All the way," said Colonel Lew Minchao, clapping. Minchao was assigned directly to Admiral Falk's staff—he and Jack would continue to interact closely, along with Maro. It was a building rather than creation from scratch, which lent some team history and continuity, even if the growing entity was still in only embryonic.

Introductions and camaraderie continued, as Falk turned the conversation to more pressing mission business. He walked to a large monitor which Jack had kept playing news feeds, which at the moment had been converted to an overhead display managed by a female Navy yeoman sitting at an equipment-laden table in the corner.

"As you have been briefed by now, this has been a Top Secret intelligence assessment mission thus far, led by our Captain Jack Dorsey. Jack, you will remain in your analyst function, but you will additionally work for me directly as unit commander of Team Gray. As such, you fill a major's slot, assisted by Captain Sepak as unit commander, and First Sergeant Boileau working with him. You will report directly to me, and work with my staff, which includes Colonel Minchao. Commander Rodriguez will be my second in command. Any questions?" He looked around the room for a minute. "If not, then we will adjourn and meet here again, same time, tomorrow morning. I will have a lot more news for you at that time. Thank you."

The gathering broke up, and Jack remained with his team.

He shook hands with Shep Sepak, the new company commander. As a military unit, the team would be commanded by Sepak, with Boileau as his first sergeant. Glancing at a hastily drawn and copied org chart from Falk's office, Jack saw he would function as field grade commander of a shadow battalion size force that might or might not form in the future. At the same time, Jack would answer directly to both Maro and her commander, Admiral Falk, with Minchao hanging off to one side in a box all his own. Like all things, this could change within the hour, but it was the orders of the day. Somehow, they would make it all work. Someone had dreamed this stuff up a long time ago. When you retired years later, you wanted to look back and say it all made sense, or at least you thought it did well enough to get the job done. That day, for Jack, was so far off in the future that it was little more than a wink and a joke today.

Jack and Shep stepped briefly outside to talk with their new chief enlisted sergeant. The exchange was brief, and classical.

Boileau waited for his two officers. While Shep vanished into the latrine for the moment, Jack walked out the door. Boileau asked one question, man to man: "What do you think?"

"I like him," Jack said meaning Falk.

"That's all we need to know," Boileau said.

The two men shook hands. Minutes later, Shep Sepak joined them and added his frivolities and personalities, and they had a few good laughs and made sincere promises to work together for the safety and success of their team.

Team Gray entered its new reality as an active duty Special Forces unit. As Boileau put it as the three leaders shared coffee later at the mess hall, "so top secret that even we don't know about it."

Jack literally burst out laughing, and nearly sputtered his coffee. Sepak and Boileau grinned broadly. They would get along well, Jack thought. Nothing to worry about. Sepak now had a new twin and shadow. Sepak and Boileau would be inseparable from here on in, as was expected of them according to military tradition.

Jack had a functioning combat team at hand, which would free him up to focus on his liaison mission with Admiral Falk and Commander Maro. Being out of the combat loop wasn't Jack's first love, but he was intrigued at being able to function at a staff level on this one, where he would be privy to a lot of juicy inside info.

For the rest of the day, Jack stayed available to the troops—including several incoming female sergeants and an officer, plus two female warrant officers, all to be led by Shep Sepak.

"Growing by leaps and bounds," Shep said as he struggled with logistics. Suddenly, where Jack's team had enjoyed their own BOQ rooms, everyone below the rank of captain now enjoyed one canvas cot low to the ground. For lack of any other facilities close by, they planned to spread the cots out in two rows at dusk, and stack them in a corner of the hangar by chow time at dawn. The several women new to the team would occupy a corner at one end, separated from the men by a hastily improvised wall of lockers brought in on a truck by mostly Malay or Philippine FNE. Within an hour, a clothes line hung across the air, with a further divider composed of gray military blankets added to the amenities. By evening, Shep Sepak had a small town going—including a coffee cart (labeled Koffee Kart in imitation of a grammar school drawing in multi-colored finger paints). They were in business.

The night passed peacefully, without much screaming in the dark.

A Shore Patrol unit appeared, consisting of male and female Navy police, to patrol the area during the night. Jack was wired up on coffee and thoughts. He needed a while to drift off, during which he was vaguely aware of a steady passage of sleepy individuals between the new barracks and their latrine—or the head, as the Navy people called what civilians normally thought of as the toilet, the bathroom, or the rest room.

13. Assignment: AFRICOM

At the next morning's early briefing, Admiral Falk had interesting news. "Welcome, everyone." Falk now had a lectern and a microphone. He was again surrounded by officers, but today there were several men and women in civilian clothing as well. "This will be the last briefing in Team Gray's billet since we will be moving this operational command to its new headquarters in the main compound. I also have this news for you. Remember, this is all top secret and when I say news, I do not mean CNN or NBC."

Everyone laughed.

"I also do not mean the cottage industry of crackpots who are raising up a storm on YouTube and social media. According to various so-called sources, Flight 777 was kidnapped by the U.S. Government for some monstrous reason that nobody has yet shared with me or with you. Allegedly, the plane is right here on the runway while aliens abduct the passengers onto a UFO. It's the international bankers, the Zionists, the Mormons, the Catholics in the Vatican, and all sorts of other lively but meaningless ideas. These people are obviously not living what Socrates was referring to when he said, about 25 centuries ago, that "The unexamined life is not worth living." Someone is making a lot of money indoctrinating these gullible souls.

"We have real business here. We have a real war here between civilization and its enemies, and for my money, we stand on the defensive perimeter between good and evil. We have a very real enemy. He is the fundamentalist, the hater of civilization, the attacker of cities, the murderer of civilized people everywhere. He wants to take us back to the stone ages, when he mistakenly believes his type of simpleton ruled. Okay, enough about that. To be sure: there are no aliens here on Diego Garcia, we have no UFOs, the Vatican has no Swiss Guards stationed here, and the United States Government is not the bad guy but the good guy. If you don't believe that, I would invite you to move to a cave somewhere, full of bats. Any takers?"

Falk waited a moment. Silence met the last echoes of his passionate speech. "I feel passionate about the nation I serve, the flag I salute, the Constitution I am sworn to uphold and protect, and the military service to which I have pledged my life. I assume that if you are here, you willingly raised your hand someplace and swore to do the same. Which is why I resent it whenever some home-grown fool makes us out to be the enemy, while we fight to uphold his right to be stupid and talk treason."

A clerk brought in a sheet of paper, which he paused to read. "Okay, with all that said, total change of gears. I am informed that this command is being transferred to the custody of the United States Africa Command, AFRICOM, whose commanding general is headquartered at Kelley Barracks in Stuttgart, Germany. We will not be integrated into their hierarchy of command and coordination, but will function as a supported command answering directly to General Marshal K. Wilson, U.S. Air Force, Commanding General of AFRICOM at Stuttgart. This gives you an appreciation of just how seriously the President of the United States, the Joint Chiefs of Staff, and the leaders of Congress and the Armed Forces take this current crisis."

Falk spoke briefly aside with some Navy technicians, then said to all: "We will hear from General Wilson shortly via satellite relay. In the meantime, in case you have not had the pleasure, I want to introduce you to my boss—the commanding officer of U.S. Naval Support Facility Diego Garcia, Captain Stuart Antonov." He handed the microphone to a tall, ramrod U.S. Navy officer in white dress uniform, who spoke briefly. Antonov welcomed all newcomers, spoke of the hospitality he hoped they would find on his base, and pledged total support. He concluded with: "I hope you will join me in understanding that the mission of uncovering what happened to Flight 777, and what our enemy intends to do with it, is now a major national priority. We can't talk about it publicly, so the crackpots will have to carry the conversation for a while, but our main concern is not who says what, but who does what. Or better yet, hopefully who is not able to do bad things to us because of your concerted efforts."

During a smattering of applause, a series of test signals flashed on all six overhead monitors. A minute later, an African-American officer's stern, fatherly visage appeared. "Good morning, Diego Garcia. This is General Wilson, newly appointed commanding general of a task force we are currently simply referring to as Operation Lima Triple. It is a very clever name, dreamed up by someone on my staff, representing three sevens turned upside down to form a row of three L's—designation Lima in military parlance. Welcome to USAFRICOM. Be assured that you have the full care and attention of my entire command structure, of U.S. Central

Command (USCENTCOM), and other Unified Combatant Commands; as well as the Joint Chiefs of Staff, and indeed your Commander in Chief. Welcome. I'll conclude my brief remarks by saying that we've received credible intelligence of a terrorist operation ongoing in a at least one African nation. Our response will be focused, measured, and appropriate. Thank you, and God Bless the United States."

After a brief silence filled the hangar, a faint ripple of applause and a few cheers and whistles crawled among some two hundred heads present.

"Aw geez," Ben Latoni muttered audibly, "I shall weep."

"Seriously, man," said Ray Marston.

"Hey guys," First Sergeant Greg Boileau said quietly, "pay attention—these guys are going to say stuff that will change your whole day."

Admiral Falk resumed the podium. "Thank you. So Operation Lima Triple is now formally under way. Sounds almost like a cocktail, doesn't it?" Laughter rose into the rafters. "I can tell you that we'll be putting boots on the ground within hours. One of our Special Forces detachments will be leaving Diego Garcia within four hours, bound for that African location General Wilson mentioned. I or my staff will conduct daily top secret briefings for your benefit. Our goal is to keep you informed so that you are at your best fighting trim. I will honestly tell you everything I know, or what they tell me, which is not always everything—but I try." He looked sheepish, and got laughs.

"Yesterday, I spelled out for you the rudiments of a command structure we are building here, ad hoc and post haste." He looked up, ever a man to quip. "That is post haste, not post waste."

Jack chuckled, as did the men and women seated on the ground around him.

"I'll take your questions on this." Falk showed a large diagram with boxes and lines sketched in. In a few minutes, with some Q&A, the tangle of military command functions was sorted out to everyone's understanding. Jack took a historian's understanding of what was happening. The military was designed like a huge, modular snap-toy set. However assembled—complete with elephantine bureaucracy and inevitable career caravans—the design intended to make the local commanders think for themselves, interpret policy on the ground, have channels to check their decisions, but act independently when needed, save lives, and get the mission accomplished.

"Needle in a haystack," Falk said, pointing to a map of Africa that appeared overhead on the large monitor. "Somewhere on that huge continent, we think sits a hijacked airliner that is being weaponized and made ready for an unknown but—I assure you—extremely painful outcome if the enemy can get away with it. The enemy? Call him Al Qaeda, Boko Haram, Baba Ganoush, call him what you will. He is the enemy of civilization. He hates buildings, people, lights, planes, music, laughter, women, children. He hates virtually everything on earth, except the charismatic stink of his divinely inspired leader. Our enemy may be an ignorant peasant who has never used a telephone, or he may be a city dweller—even a doctor, a lawyer, a teacher—who has had a sudden conversion to extremism for reasons that are beyond my pay grade. Let the psychiatrists figure out where all that hate comes from or what it means. It is classic cult programming. The individual becomes isolated from the mainstream of society and becomes part of a hypnotic cult. They are immersed in a culture of constant repetition of a few driving mantras, songs, scripture verses taken out of context. They are subjected to a constant stream of misinformation or disinformation that breaks them down, removes what little critical thinking apparatus they may have had, and leaves them to spout slogans and look forward to sacrificing themselves for the cause. Like drug addicts, they become insanely addicted to this adrenalin rush, and stay plugged in by day and night. The light at the end of their tunnel is an onrushing train—death—theirs, and as many people's as they can take with them when they throw their lives away. This is nothing new. The world has seen this kind of fanatical group thinking since the beginning of civilization. It's the anti-civilization, if you will. We are not here to abstract or analyze, however. We do need to understand enough to assess our enemy.

"I give you one fact. Their murder spree on 9/11 cost about 3,000 lives. It's been well over a decade. We have stopped a lot of their often crude plots. We've taken some more hits, like the train bombing in Madrid or the bus bombing in London, and others. We killed their leader, Osama bin Laden. The anniversary of his killing is at hand once more. Be assured that they are actively working on revenge, and not only that—they have to outdo 9/11. So how do they do that? They have to pull off something far more horrible and spectacular than hitting the Pentagon or bringing down the Twin

Towers. They want to kill a lot more people this time around. And they have to do it in a way that will make us all grit our teeth, tear our hair, and grow terrified. That is their message, their only reason for existing in their pitiful meaningless lives, and their only mission in a life they hate and cannot wait to throw away. To hit us again, to hit us with a blaze and surprise where we least expect it, and to impress the world. Our enemy is desperate, because they have not been able to set the world on fire. Their cause is already long ago lost. They just don't know it yet. We have to cut off their avenues of action, starting right here. Theirs is a lost cause, my friends. They have lost all credibility with the sane, decent people who really matter for effect. There are some smug, dirty little creatures around the world in business suits, with expensive watches and bank accounts, who secretly applaud, but are too cowardly to show their duplicity or pettiness. They don't count either. It always comes down to you folks, the warriors in a just cause, and the people of all countries who love their families and support you." Falk pointed to a region on the monitor as the map zoomed in closer. He pointed with a yard stick. "That, ladies and gentlemen, is the northeastern quarter of Africa. You see how Africa is shaped roughly like a skull looking east. It looks almost like the skull of one of our primitive ancestors long ago. Along the top is North Africa, along the Mediterranean Sea, stretching from Gibraltar in the west, along the southern rim of Europe including Spain, France, Italy, and the Balkans including Hellas and Turkey, all the way to western Asia. That's what we used to call the Near East, until the world changed. Today, everything is so close, within hours of air travel, that near doesn't mean anything relative to anything else. We are all near each other on one tiny little planet.

"If you look along the coast of North Africa, it is like the top of the skull. Its mostly large nations share beaches giving direct access to the Mediterranean Sea. We have Morocco, Algeria, Tunisia, Libya, and Egypt from west to east. Hang on to that thought for a moment until I come around again." He moved his pointer down the western, or left, or South Atlantic coast of Africa.

"Along the South Atlantic, you see the back of the cranium sticking out. That is called West Africa, and includes a lot of countries including Ivory Coast, Togo, and Mauritania. Like most of the northern tier, it is all mostly desert and mountains.

"You see a belt of greenery across the continent at the Equator. That is Equatorial Africa, which includes the nations of Congo, Democratic Republic of Congo, and Central African Republic.

"The lower third of Africa tapers down into some fertile forest countries and eventually the temperate regions of South Africa. None of that is currently our focus of concern.

"I said I would come around, and here I am. At the top right of the map, we see Libya and Egypt. As in much of the region, there have been years of unrest as various factions fight for political control. Typically, you have the old style military juntas in these Arab states, most of which were at one time Soviet clients. You also have modern, progressive forces that seek democracy and Western-style economic growth. Finally, you have the sorts of cave men who want to return everyone to their private hell, as exemplified by the horrible brutality of the Taliban when they ruled Afghanistan, or various Al Qaeda type terror groups that have attempted to rule countries around the region.

"Let's focus in on two main areas of concern. I'll try to keep a complex situation simple. We are left with two areas.

"The first of these is the Horn of Africa, which is that piece sticking out just below the Arabian Peninsula, on the Red Sea. That includes, among other things, the notorious region known as Somalia, which is still today one of the most lawless places on earth. It is one of the few places with a name that is not actually a nation.

"The second area of concern is what we are calling, for purposes of this mission, our main area of concern—the Sudan Tangent. That includes what was until recently Africa's largest country, a very ancient one, the Sudan. It is ruled by a relatively unstable Islamic government that tries to rule by a mix of corruption, military force, brutality, and Islamic extremism under Sharia law.

"Surrounding this, and part of our Sudan Tangent, are large chunks of surrounding nations. I will reserve mentioning South Sudan, the world's newest country, until the end of my talk.

"Tangent regions include desert portions of Chad and Libya in the northwest, as well as highland savannah and broken terrain in northern Central African Republic, and a portion of the Democratic Republic of Congo. These are all nations with long histories of civil war and instability following colonial rule which ended half a century ago.

"I can tell you that, as for now, we have ruled out Somalia, Puntland, and Somaliland as possible staging points for our enemy, where we think they may be hiding and fitting out this hijacked aircraft for a strike against a civilized target somewhere to the north.

"One last item before I turn to the specifics of our mission. This is really important to clarify. There has been a long history of Chinese involvement in the drilling and export of oil in the South Sudan region. I want to emphasize: we do not believe that China has any connection with the Flight 777 incident. They have nothing to gain from the turmoil this situation is starting to create and actually they have much to lose. They are not a major oil producer, but they are now a huge energy consumer. They rely on a stable supply of coal and oil around the world more than most nations. It is worth noting that South Sudan declared independence from the north a few years ago, taking with them the major sources of Sudan's rich oil reserves. The north remains the corrupt, brutal Sharia dictatorship it was before. They were notorious for enabling one of the world's last major slave trading economies, while waging incessant war on their Christian and Animist majorities in the south. Big surprise then that the south finally broke away, with the support of much of the civilized world. My main purpose in mentioning any of this is to simply make you aware that the government in Beijing has serious, heavy interests invested in this area, and I imagine we will have folks from Washington briefing folks from Beijing around the clock in both our capitals as to whatever is going on. Any questions?" Admiral Falk waited, looking around the hangar for any raised hands. "Good. Then you understand everything. Better than I do, I'm sure. Now to the exciting part. Let's zoom in our maps and satellite images a bit."

Jack watched as the northeastern section of the Central African Republic (C.A.R.) floated up toward eye level on the monitors.

Falk said: "This is C.A.R.. Like Somalia, it's virtually a failed nation. We have sharp satellite imagery, meaning that you are looking at a picture so clear—seen from orbit with no cloud cover, in broad daylight on a day with low relative humidity—that it's like looking at an object one foot away. I know it looks like your mother's herb garden back home, seen through a magnifying glass. As your eyes focus, you'll see that we are looking at a forest clearing. The area here is not so much jungle but savannah, with nice lush stands of deciduous trees and lots of leaves. I think that

white dot over there in one corner is even a deer, temporarily
looking away while it farts for our camera." *Laughter*. "Sorry. I like
to lighten the gloom a bit whenever I can. Lurking down in those
woods may be all sorts of unpleasant people, including the
cannibals and murderers we've seen over the years in places like
Liberia and in fact C.A.R.—including the former emperor,
Bokassa, who once hosted some European leaders to a dinner of
human and monkey flesh—that was the rumor. There may be bush
fighters, or Islamic folks, or other people with agendas. Typically,
the bush folks like to run around the jungle or the forest hunting in
peace. Along come the farmer types, who may be Christians, who
ruin the whole day by fencing off the land. To make matters more
complicated, along come some Arabized Islamic fellows in Soviet-
style tanks, racing around to protect their fellow ethnics who tend to
be herdsmen—who hate fences and farms, just like in the Old Wild
West in the United States—oops, maybe still today in places. It's
not an African problem, but a human problem, a historic problem,
with sociological and anthropological aspects.

"Regard the image again. See an area that looks faintly rusty or
discolored? Folks, that is several hundred square feet of camouflage
cover. We've had planes fly over it, and ping it with all sorts of
gadgets, and hiding under there is a large metal object with white
surface paint and red stripes. Experts think our missing aircraft is
sitting underneath there. Look more closely."

Falk pointed with his yard stick. "We call this Camp Zero. You
see what looks like a two mile road surface through that clearing.
Analysts tell us that would be the runway our plane needs to get
airborne. Further hidden in the brush, you see some objects that
might be fuel trucks. Our intelligence specialists have studied these
images in close detail, and determined that we need to fly a unit of
commandos in there right now—wasting no time—and ruin those
folks' entire day for them." He put the pointer aside. "We already
have a SEAL team on the way from Djibouti, and the French have a
French Foreign Legion detachment airborne as we speak, ready to
drop by parachute within a few hours. Kenya has pathfinder troops
in the field to secure a landing zone. The military operation to take
Camp Zero is underway. For our part, we are sending our own
Team Gray to join the effort to secure this area and end the
nightmare of the vanished Flight 777."

Part Three: African Mission

14.   Commandos on the ground

Jack was summoned to a personal meeting with Admiral Paul Falk in his operational headquarters, which occupied a recently constructed row of concrete-block buildings near the twin runways.

Jack chose to walk the one mile by himself. The company of Maro or one of his team would have been nice, but everyone was suddenly busy, and Jack felt a need for some time alone, given the close quarters.

Shep Sepak and Greg Boileau were hustling to get two dozen troops ready for action. These were divided into a Team A and a Team B. The women were in Team B, which was to provide rear echelon support at a staging area near Camp Zero, while Team A went in by helicopter (provided by the French) to support the already forward Legionnaires and SEALs as well as Nigerian and Kenyan pathfinders.

At sea all around the coral atoll, Jack could see the gray shapes of aircraft and ships in motion. The entire U.S. and Allied military machine was in full operation.

Back home in San Diego County, Catherine was having contractions. Jack's sister Janet lived permanently on the large family ranch in Temecula with her husband, geologist Mark Barger. With their parents now deceased, Jack and Janet co-owned the ranch. They got along well. Jack also had a house in San Diego, close to downtown, but tucked away on a palm tree-laced mesa overlooking the sea from Mission Cliffs. Catherine stayed with the Bargers whenever Jack was away on Reserve duty, like now. On the way to Falk's HQ, Jack spoke with Catherine and Janet via cell and satellite relay. "Honey, don't worry," came Catherine's sweet voice from a balcony, which Jack imagined as overlooking San Diego Bay at Balboa Naval Hospital. "Millions of women have premature contractions. Don't you worry. Are you eating right?"

"Yeah," he said, grinning. "Everything is just fine, honey. You be brave and do your job over there, okay?"

"I am doing the best I can, with help from Sis."

"I'm glad. I can relax and not have a nervous breakdown."

"Honey, be strong," she said half jokingly. "Have courage. Everything is going to go down just fine. This was just a false alarm. You'll be a daddy in no time, don't worry. I'm not due for another six weeks. Enjoy the peace and quiet while it lasts."

"You do the same, baby." He spoke briefly with Janet, asked about Mark and the ranch, and rang off. He felt grounded and at peace as long as he know all was well on the home front.

Paul Falk saw Jack privately in his office on the second floor of a plain white building overlooking a soccer field. "Sit down, Jack."

"Thank you, Sir."

"Coffee?" Falk waved a carafe from a cupboard near his office window, which overlooked a strip of jungle canopy.

"No thanks. I'm all caffeinated already this morning."

"I know the feeling." Falk poured himself a steaming cup, black, that filled the room with an acrid aroma. After carefully setting the cup down, he threw himself into his high-backed chair and swiveled half a turn from the impact. "You've done well, Jack. Thanks for your insights. I keep wondering—how can an entire world full of people be looking at a missing plane in the Indian Ocean, and fail to notice the continent of Africa staring at them from the left corners of their eyeballs?"

Jack shrugged. "Hard to guess, Sir. Still the dark continent—the unknown, the unknowable."

Falk winced as he sipped from his coffee cup. "So now, Jack, assuming we have the plane, what next? We need to make sure nothing like this happens again."

"Sounds like a job for the FAA and a lot of other civilian organizations—internationally."

"Of course. I mean not letting Iranian men with stolen European passports board international flights. I mean not letting garage monkeys preposition explosives in fuselage doors. Beyond that, I'm talking about going after the planners, wherever they may be. Got any insights on that?"

Jack sat with his hands knotted between his knees. After a minute, he said: "I've thought about it, and the best thing I come up with is that there must be a global terrorism organization at work. Maybe it's just Arabs, or a bigger net involving Muslims, but I just wonder. Someone could make a lot of money at this."

"Russian mafia, maybe?"

"Chechens? Drug lords who already have the infrastructure? Good question. There is already global trafficking in drugs, in weapons, and in human slaves for sex or labor."

Falk said: "You mean like free market economics. Create some demand, and business will follow."

"Yes," Jack said. "So if I were in a position to fight it—I mean, like presidential level—I might organize a sting."

"Using the CIA, the FBI, Interpol, that kind of thing?"

"Yessir."

Falk nodded. He stared into the air above Jack's head, as if considering something; then he looked directly at Jack. "Been to Paris lately?"

Jack shrugged. "In and out. I spent a year in Heidelberg, working on my Master's in History. That's a few years ago."

Falk sat forward, holding the cup on the desk between both hands. "I'm told we have a lead on the people who sold the stolen passports."

"Really. That's interesting."

"Some Algerian black market thugs tried to solicit a British undercover agent for a stolen identity deal in Marly-le-Roi. U.K.'s MI6 turned it over to the Deuxieme Bureau, which is essentially French civilian G-2."

"Got it. And you are telling me because why?"

"Keep thinking outside the box, Jack. I know you like the boots on the ground stuff. Hiking, yodeling, shooting, camping—great stuff. But you are an analytical thinker, and your skills are needed in the bigger realm of things."

"Military intelligence?"

"That, or the Foreign Service, the CIA. Keep your Reserve commission, get your Ph.D., and come see me. I'll give you a good reference, and some people to go visit."

Jack stared at his boss. "You wear a lot of hats, I take it."

"I am a regular hat rack."

"Sure, that sounds interesting."

"If you tell anyone about my hats, I'll deny everything. You have talent. Keep our conversation in mind, okay?"

"I will. Thank you." Jack found the vaguely worded offer, if that it was, intriguing. He had a feeling he'd mull it over, and talk to Admiral Falk again some day.

"In the meantime, getting back to earth—sort of literally—I am hoping we can mop up this plane thing in the next few days. I have a gut feeling the State Department will end up making an announcement once we successfully wrap things up."

"We keep Team Gray under wraps."

"Right, Jack. I wouldn't give our enemy ideas that they haven't already had. Let them think we are dumber than we really are."

Jack grinned. "It's a UFO story."

"The Evil Government," Falk said with a nasty grin.

"The Vatican," Jack said.

"Organize all the information for me, now that we have a handle on this situation. Brief me daily, so that I can brief AFRICOM, so they can promptly pass word up or along the chain to other entities—including CENTCOM, NATO, the Joint Chiefs of Staff, and Congress. It's a food chain, and we are sardines. We feed the tuna, who feed the sharks and whales, and so forth."

Jack rose. "I'll start pulling it together."

"Talk to my master chief petty officer outside. She will coordinate with your Navy contact, Commander Rodriguez. You will have some office space on this floor by tomorrow. Start living here, okay?"

"Yessir."

"I know you'll miss being with your team. Let's support them the best we can."

As he left, Jack had mixed feelings at letting go of his daily operational ties with Team Gray, the Coconut Project. He'd miss Ben and Ray. It was a bit like letting go of Robert Keaka, who lived on in his heart. However, Falk sounded as if he expected to wrap up Operation Lima Triple soon. He'd return to mainstream duties—an ambitious, capable man, always in motion, taking care of business while planning ahead for his own career. No doubt he had strong mentors up the chain, because he had that privileged air. He was a mix of derring-do pilot and fair-haired lad—but he was for real. Every organization had its charmed climbers. You couldn't help but like and admire a guy like Falk, and follow his progress with approval. Someone had to do it.

When Jack returned to the hangar two hours later, he found a strangely hollow atmosphere. The place had a deserted feeling. The A and B Teams had been flown out on short notice with full gear, loaded onto a C-17 headed for Nairobi, Kenya, where the U.S. and her allies had a footprint.

He bumped into Colonel Lew Minchao, who had stopped by, wearing freshly purchased fatigues and boots (not yet shined), to coordinate some quartermaster issues. Along with him came Maro, who was on some admin mission, putting together a pool of clerks from various services. Feeling a bit left out, Jack wandered off to the nearby building that housed foreign intelligence analysts including Rebekah Goldstein of the IDF and Mustafa ibn Malik (Don). Rebekah was gone for the day. Don sat in his office dictating a report in Arabic to a man wearing a dark business suit and, on his head, a white *ghutrah* with a black cord or *agal*. Don's counsel was: "It's not over until it's over, Jack. Keep a pot of coffee on the back burner." Jack sighed deeply. Don might mix his metaphors, but his heart was in the right place, along with his coffee beans. As a man of action, Jack realized it would take some doing to switch gears and become a man of words—to become Admiral Falk's staff reporter, so to speak. Where to start? What to do? As he pondered, his cell phone rang. He took it from his pocket and raised it to his ear. "Yes?"

"Jack." It was the distant, distorted voice of Ben Latoni.

"Hey," Jack said. "How are you?"

"Jack," Ben said, or yelled, before the phone connection went dead. In the background, Jack heard about a tenth of a second of loud noise that could be anything from Ben falling over a pile of hubcaps to a rattle of large caliber machine gun fire to the end of the world. Or just static.

Jack pressed the pre-dial for Falk's office. "Sir, I just had a strange phone call from one of my men. Not sure what is going on."

Falk said tersely: "You'd better get over to my office ASAP. All hell is breaking loose over in Africa."

"I'm on my way," Jack said, and started running along the palm tree lined concrete path connecting the air strip with the new admin block. Somewhere, a klaxon started to cry out in hoarse, short stabbing cries that echoed across the tranquility of Diego Garcia. Sirens began to howl in deep, mournful, horrible tones, up and down, that echoed for miles.

Jack could see more people running in the distance, and air traffic boiled up in a hornet's nest on the runways as Diego Garcia unexpectedly huffed into emergency mode.

The men and women of Operation Lima Triple (the expanded version of Ben and Ray's Operation Coco Nuts) flew into Nairobi's Jomo Kenyatta International Airport on a U.S. Air Force C-17 Globemaster III. The massive, stubby, functionally elegant transport plane crawled to a landing at the Kenyan Air Force facility on the north runway, known as Old Embakasi Airport. This was not only a main operational hub for the Kenyan military, but also a gateway for certain U.N. and African Union international military peace keeping missions. Handling of the huge U.S. cargo plane was therefore routine by the competent military technical staff at Embakasi, which suited Admiral Falk's planners and his AFRICOM chain of command.

On board were Captain Shep Sepak, his First Sergeant Greg Boileau, plus the original two NCOs at the core of Operation Coconut, Master Sergeants Ben Latoni and Ray Marston. With them on Team A were six other men, including the new XO (Executive Officer), a weapons warrant officer grade one, and two sergeants.

Also traveling with them were the ten members of Team B, who would follow closely and maintain logistical and base camp operations, but not engage in direct combat. These were an evenly mixed group of male and female NCOs and warrant officers, including two physician assistants and two medical technicians.

From Nairobi, both teams immediately embarked on a British C-130 with a detachment of Special Air Services troops who would be joining the French brigade that was already on the ground in C.A.R..

As Shep and his people learned, the various regional powers, including the eastern African community of nations, U.N. peace keeping forces, and other alliances, had cleared the multinational operation so that its forces could cross borders officially without hindrance. That did not include assurances from the many rebel and bandit groups that operated with lawless abandon at will—for example, ambushing innocent girls drawing water at river sides, raping them, and mutilating—and worse with young boys they captured. The terrain below was as beautiful and hypnotic as it could be hellish and horrifying. It was the kind of landscape in which the Flight 777 hijackers would naturally find themselves comfortable and at home.

One of the female warrants had a Ph.D. in geography, though her reserve duty was as a physician assistant. She kept everyone occupied (and happy) by lecturing as she sat beside an open bay door, strapped in comfortably on a pile of soft sea or duffel bags, and held a small hand microphone. A variety of sunny vistas floated steadily past, as her voice modulated pleasantly above the drone of the engines. Patches of cloud floated past not far below. Generally, the landscape below was heavily forested, but receding into grassland on the northern horizon as they flew westward. Occasionally they passed over large lakes, sparkling swamp lands, and glittering rivers. From time to time, she paused to point out clusters of animals watering below, especially herds of broad-horned cattle. One could not see them, but the landscape also included crocodiles, hippos, giraffes, elephants, lions, and other fabulous, mostly endangered fauna.

The Equator—an imaginary line drawn around the earth, upon which the distance between the earth and the sun is at its least as the planet rotates through the day—lay upon much of the scenario of Operation Lima Triple. The Equator passes through both Congo republics, the Central African Republic, Uganda, Kenya, and Somalia. The Equator passes near the Maldives, where the missing Malaysian airliner was spotted by a fisherman in the early hours of March 8th, and through Indonesia—not far from Malaysia, where Flight 777 coincidentally originated.

Now the small air armada heading for a showdown with terrorists flew over Lake Victoria in Uganda—a nation still gripped in cruelty and turmoil—into the Congo region. The airplanes stayed close to the northern border between the strife-torn Democratic Republic of Congo and the world's newest nation, South Sudan, which was just beginning to recover from generations of bloody sectarian strife.

Shep Sepak, a former University of Iowa running back and long distance bicycling champion, was an ROTC officer with a Bachelor of Science in Mechanical Engineering. He had been commissioned as an engineer officer, but had volunteered for unconventional warfare and now found himself leading a mission in the heart of Africa.

Leading the plane were two Chinese-made Harbin Y-12 transports of the Kenyan Air Force. The dun-colored twin-engine turboprops were slow, sturdy, and reliable—comparable to Canada's ubiquitous DeHavilland Twin Otter, the classic puddle jumper of North American wilderness areas, but also a standard small passenger plane.

As one of the two pilots on board the C-130 explained, the Chinese had been selling military hardware in Africa for decades as they slowly built an economic and political presence. China is now the world's largest energy user, importing more oil than any other nation—and desperate to maintain stable supplies of fuel outside volatile Arab channels.

On board the C-130, filling its cavernous hold, were about thirty troops including the commandos of Operation Lima Triple, plus four lightly armored, highly mobile vehicles to transport them. Each vehicle featured a medium-caliber machine gun mounted on a roof turret, plus a veritable Swiss Army Knife of attachments including small satellite dishes, tool stands for quick jungle repairs, and more.

Within hours, the three aircraft traveled from the general region of eastern Africa into the general region of central Africa. They traveled along the border between Democratic Republic of Congo (D.R.C.) and the Central African Republic (C.A.R.), in the northern reaches of the Congo River basin. The southern portion of C.A.R. is deep equatorial jungle, like the rest of the Congo basin, while the northern parts of the country consist primarily of open grassland or savanna. World-wide, this type of vegetation is broadly classified as grasslands, scrublands, or savanna—including such regions as the North American prairies, South American pampas, and the vast Eurasian steppes famous for their Mongol conquerors. The entire spectrum of grassy lands covers at least one fifth of the Earth's land area. As the warrant officer explained, they were in a relatively narrow transitional band between the equatorial rainforests of the Congo basin to the south, and the gradually sparser grasslands to the north, leading further into the deserts identified with the nations of Sudan and Chad hundreds of miles to the north and away from the Equator.

Evidently the hijackers of Flight 777 had chosen a dense stretch of jungle in southern C.A.R., bordering on the D.R.C..

Shep, Greg, and their commando teams landed at a relatively small town in the south central region of the Central African Republic, called Bambari. This is the small capital (43,000 inhabitants) of Ouaka Prefecture. As with many towns in the region, it is rich in minerals and other natural resources. It is dotted with ruins from past efforts to mine or otherwise extract this wealth—but has been ravaged by civil war and mismanagement. Foreign investors have included the Australians, the Chinese, the French, British, and U.S., but most have abandoned their buildings, hospitals, and air strips. The one persistent regional power have been the South Africans, who are closer to the problem. Their corporations have much to gain. Like the French in northerly areas, the South Africans know how to navigate among war lords and the craziest of the sectarian militias like the Lords' Resistance Army out of Uganda, and various other pseudo-religious, armed murder mobs led by petty tyrants who come and go.

This seemed like the perfect area for a lawless hideout of Flight 777 hijackers—or so thought the distant overlords of AFRICOM.

C.A.R.'s air force was virtually nonexistent, so French Dassault Mirage F1-family air superiority fighters patrolled the skies. Given the country's colonial ties with France (ended with independence and chaos in the 1960s), France was the front line European power called upon to restore some semblance of order in this borderline failed nation, not the only one in transitional Africa.

France is a natural ex-colonial heavy in the region. The French Foreign Legion was created in the 1830s by the French crown as a way of keeping ex-Napoleonic generals busy and away from European affairs—by occupying them with the struggle for conquest in North Africa. While the British empire focused on coastal coaling stations in Africa and around the world, the Germans, the French, and other colonial aspirants sought the mineral riches of the interior. The Germans twice met their demise on 20th Century battlefields of Europe. The French maintained some grasp on their fading colonial empires of the mid-20th Century, including impoverished and newly created nation states of Africa, by tradition often tribal rather than national.

As various instructors informed Shep Sepak and his troops on the route into the Bambari district, the operation to recover Flight 777 was being carried out with the tacit agreement of regional powers, but with a primarily foreign command structure. This was to maintain tactical surprise and speed, as well as simplicity. Kenyan and Tanzanian pathfinder troops were the primary theater troops involved. Everything else was staged by Europeans and their allies in the U.S. and elsewhere. The operation was strictly a flashing, arrow head strike, aiming to decapitate a rogue enemy thought to have infested the area like a foreign disease organism.

Aiding the speed and stealth of the French and AFRICOM led strike force was the silence of the perpetrators themselves. This would soon give rise to a new dimension in terror, but the world was as yet blissfully unaware of the patience, brilliance, and resilience of this global foe. The enemy was utterly ruthless, self-assured, and bolstered with Mahdist fanaticism rooted in belief systems far more ancient than Islam—animist strains of ritual and belief that caused men to practice cannibalism and believe that drinking human blood made them impervious to bullets or harm.

In a secret jungle valley south of Bambari, pathfinders had staked out a base camp of the unknown enemy who had hijacked Flight 777. The trackers readily identified the men at the base camp as Muslims. In fact, cell phone recordings broadcast to remote tracking stations, and relayed to Western intelligence agencies, suggested a mixture of Chechen, Malaysian, and local African languages being spoken, with smatterings of more distant tongues.

Jack Dorsey and his team on Diego Garcia would piece all this together in the hours and days to come.

In the pre-dawn hours of a tropical day in early May, the assault on Camp Zero began. This operation remained totally unknown to a world that was already starting to lose interest in the mysteriously vanished airliner. Search and recovery efforts continued in the southern Indian Ocean off the coast of Australia. Far-out conspiracy theorists launched a cult of supernatural and apocalyptic ideations in the absence or fact, logic, information, and common sense.

On a saner note—based on air and ground reconnaissance in the past week—allied planners estimated the number of terrorists at Camp Zero to be between thirty and ninety. That included perhaps thirty Chechens and Malaysians who had refitted the plane in the Bay of Bengal and then flown on to C.A.R., plus another thirty to sixty Ugandan or Sudanese militia members.

A drone had flown overhead, carefully assessing the situation while U.S., British, and French experts analyzed the footage. It seemed clear: the enemy had made one slight error in covering the aircraft with camouflage netting of a slightly inappropriate coloration. Instead of dark and light greens for the tropical forest, the strips of cloth loosely woven into the similarly colored, braided nylon rope were more appropriate for autumn forest colors in a temperate region like Western Europe or eastern U.S.A. Seen from orbit by satellite imaging, there appeared to be an anomaly amid the jungle canopy, verging into russets and yellows. Not only that, but electronic signal pinging revealed a heavy metallic, cruciform aircraft shape underneath. Everything fit the expected profile.

Operation Lima Triple had found their missing aircraft—so everyone thought.

Toward dawn, three large troop-carrying helicopters carrying French Foreign Legionnaires in full combat gear roared in low over the jungle canopy from a staging area fifty miles away. On cue, African pathfinders melted away in to the jungle after hiding out in the bush for days, observing activities at Camp Zero.

Shep Sepak and Team A detached from the rest of their unit at Bambari and roared toward Camp Zero aboard a large Chinook CH-47 helicopter capable of carrying nearly 40 troops and their gear. Meanwhile, two other Chinooks roared in from other directions—one carrying a detachment of U.S. Navy SEALs, the other a detachment of British Special Air Services troops who had been in training with South African forces in that nation. In all, over 200 specialized troops were to make a lightning strike on Camp Zero within the hour. When the area was locked down, they would be followed by more U.S. and European troops, plus 2,000 African Union infantry from Kenya, Tanzania, and Ethiopia.

For the first twenty minutes, the landing went smoothly and the operation appeared to be going smoothly.

Shep Sepak and Greg Boileau, with their half dozen men including Ben Latoni and Ray Marston, seized a hilltop strategically overlooking the small plateau valley in which the camouflaged aircraft was hidden. Team A set up a radio relay, secured a perimeter, and began a tactical overlook of the valley from their position. Shep squatted in a blind of palm leaves and held a receiver to each ear as he communicated with his French counterpart, a *Légion étrangère* captain, on one side and his British counterpart, a British Army S.A.S. major, on the other.

For a moment, everything seemed clear. Shep could see the long, straight line of a hard-packed dirt road stretching into the hazy distance as it slashed diagonally across the valley. Presumably, the aircraft would roll out, make a half turn, and roar away into the air on a two mile runway created by the road.

The Chinook helicopters rattled by at about 2,500 feet in a clear, powder-blue sky marred only by some high, snowy, harmless cirrus clouds. Passing out of small arms range, the choppers began dropping rows of dots that turned into billowing, fast-moving paragliders. Each guided parachute executed sharp, evasive turns as the French airborne detachment quickly found their way to earth on a landscape of rolling grassland punctuated by small hillocks of brush and trees. It was open country, but tactically defensible with nearby forest cover. The troopers ran from their chutes and high-tailed it into the brush, all within a few minutes of jumping.

Shep Sepak left Ben Latoni and Ray Marston to handle the field radios while he watched through high-powered binoculars. In the distance, he watched the other Chinooks set down, disgorging U.S. and British troops before roaring away in to the sky.

Ten minutes into the operation, Shep was exchanging puzzled commentary with the French and British commanders. Oddly, there was no resistance on the ground. What had happened to the thirty to ninety terrorist fighters they had expected to be exchanging fire with by now? Pathfinders with binoculars, hiding like snipers, had watched the enemy as Chechens and southeast Asians moved among their tents, and wandered in and out of the cloth hanger hiding the weaponized plane.

Fifteen minutes into the operation, the allied troops on the ground numbered over 100. They had seized about a dozen high points, including the hilltop on which Shep and his team held fast.

On a twenty minute mark whistle from an NCO, a skirmish line of FFL soldiers carefully made their way point to point across the broken ground running slightly uphill toward the camouflage netting covering the metallic shape observed from orbit.

There was total silence except for the screech and flutter of passing birds. A gentle wind luffed in the rigging of the camo circus. This was an expansive structure about 400 feet in diameter, roughly forming a square with rounded corners as seen from space.

Shep spoke with his French contact. "Approach with caution."

"It has the smell of an ambush," the Frenchman agreed. "We have the high ground front and back."

The British officer on the line added: "We can't see a soul. I think they ran."

Shep got a strange feeling in his gut. Beside him, Ben Latoni said: "Sir, what if it's an ambush of some kind?"

Shep did not know what to say. "I don't know, Ben. I guess we will know more once we get people into the tent and secure what's underneath there."

A point team of French pioneers carried with them a video camera to film whatever they encountered.

Walking carefully, two squads of FFL troops in heavy gear and camouflage uniforms slowly entered the shadows of the huge dome under which the satellites had detected a metallic aircraft shape. At the point of the FFL team was a technician holding a large video recorder with both arms. It rested on his right shoulder, and he was just twisting its lenses up front to adjust them to the gloom. He remarked in surprise when he saw what was under the dome.

Shep gasped as he saw a crude array of metal sheds, boxes, sheet metal, and other junk piled around the rusting hulk of a long-dead C.A.R. military aircraft—perhaps the one and only C-130 that a former corrupt president had purchased for his private amusement in the absence of any law, order, or national unity.

Flight 777 had never been here. It was a trap.

Admiral Falk and his staff including Jack Dorsey, and in Stuttgart the staff of General Wilson, all witnessed what happened next—after an hour's delay, once video reached Diego Garcia.

All hell broke loose.

In several dozen spots, the ground lifted up in coordinated, rolling waves.

At first, there was silence as a shock wave the color of white smoke streaked in all directions within a few meters above the ground.

Seconds later, a deafening roar filled the air.

Shep blacked out for a few seconds as he was thrown upward, spinning, and landed on the ground. The air was filled with red and black flashes as prepositioned land mine explosives went off throughout the valley. The air was filled with flying clods of dirt, broken tree limbs, rocks, pieces of people and equipment, and dead birds killed in mid-flight.

The lumpy dome shape, a camouflage lure colored russet and yellow like a New England autumn forest, flew apart as more than a thousand pounds of high explosives rigged for maximum impact went into the air—along with a diabolical assortment of shrapnel including steel pegs, nails, knotted bits of wire, and anything else the enemy had time to rig up during the lost time leading up to the disaster of Camp Zero.

The lifeless body of Ray Marston lay sprawled nearby.

Shep felt his mouth full of blood and dirt as he crawled on all fours, shaking his head to clear it. One of the explosives had gone off nearby, deafening him. He had no idea if he was dying or if he had been spared by a tree trunk or other cover.

He heard Ben Latoni on his cell phone, calling out to Jack Dorsey back on Diego Garcia. Then a flying object struck Ben on the helmet, knocking him down and spattering the cell phone as it was knocked from his hand.

As he blacked out, Shep's one thought was that, if he enemy were waiting to strike under cover of surprise, they'd be just as overwhelmed by the massive explosions rocking the valley. Shep made peace as the ground rushed up toward his face, and darkness closed in.

As Jack Dorsey ran toward the blockhouse building he could hear shouting. Something terrible had happened in Africa, if Ben Latoni's abortive cell call was any indication.

Sprinting up the concrete interior stairs with their metal tube railings, he could hear Falk yelling hoarsely, over and over: "What happened? What happened? Somebody tell me what just happened."

As Jack entered the offices on the second floor, he found pale faces bent over computers and desk phones. Uniformed men and women on Falk's staff were starting to react to the disastrous news out of C.A.R.

The strike force had been crippled on the ground, if not outright wiped out. Paul Falk, a directive ball of energy as always, was at the center of his own private hurricane as the pieces of his command whirled in the air around his head.

With his own team gone to Africa—and likely lost—Jack felt an unreal sensation as if the ground had been torn away from underneath him. He could certainly understand Falk's frenzied effort to stabilize a torpedoed and sinking ship. For a half hour, all Jack could do was to stand amid chaos as men and women rushed about. Orders came from Germany, from Washington, from Africa. Data flowed from around the world—more questions than information.

Within an hour, Falk's staff were sorting through an avalanche *communiqués* requiring the admiral's attention. The base commander of Diego Garcia, U.S. Navy Captain Antonov, arrived with a horde of technicians and bureaucrats, in uniform and not, to help sort through the message traffic and consternation.

Bit by bit, status on the shattered assault force began to emerge. They were too far from civilization to effect immediate answers or rescue. However, a few facts became clear. Shep Sepak's Team B were airlifted out of Bambari with a planeload of local medical staff. The African Union had a field hospital in the northern part of D.R.C., from which they sent a half dozen doctors and nurses via a Canadian-built Bombardier CRJ100 cargo transport. The French had a field hospital in the region, which was now on standby to receive casualties. The French Foreign Legion had a medical unit attached, which had survived the ambush and was treating casualties in an open field environment. The Ethiopian air force had a medical evacuation plane in the air from Addis Ababa, scheduled to arrive at Bambari within the next few hours. A full international rescue effort was underway—too late to save many of the wounded. Admiral Falk had an information room set up, dedicated to receiving minute by minute updates from Bambari and Camp Zero.

Diplomats in Washington and in African capitals were beginning to sort out the matter of protest notes about the foreign invasion of C.A.R.—which was being treated as an issue related to mining. The South Africans were taking the brunt of it, having volunteered to stand as patsies for the next few weeks on the assumption that they had somehow gotten into a brawl with the French (and of course, what else, the U.S.) over uranium mining.

Rebekah Goldstein and Mustafa 'Donald' ibn Malik showed up to lend their governments' support. "It is important to suppress the real nature of the raid," Goldstein said; "if still possible." Her doubt was prescient, as it turned out.

Don concurred. "The world needs to remain baffled about the situation with Flight 777. We cannot hand the extremists a propaganda victory—especially not with the way they set us all up for this ambush in C.A.R.."

Jack was betwixt and between. His team were gone, and the hangar seemed like an eerie, ghostly reminder of their fate—which was unknown as yet. No word from Ben Latoni, Ray Marston, Greg Boileau, or Shep Sepak as yet. Jack hoped to receive word soon from support troops of Team B as they set up shop near Camp Zero and sorted through casualties. Jack now had a desk and a chair and a phone down the hall from Admiral Falk's suite of offices—but nothing to do there except hold a séance or a wake with Rebekah and Donald. *To hell with that.* Furiously, Jack went for a solitary walk along the beach. As he stumbled through the wet sand, sometimes soaked by incoming waves, his eyes filled with tears. Had he been wrong? Had he led the entire operation into a trap? Was he the biggest fool on earth? Should he blame himself?

For a while, he sat on a boulder overlooking the empty sea, and thought of his wife and family back home. Were they all right? Gradually, he calmed down. He resisted the urge to call Catherine. She must not hear him in this condition. He stood on the boulder, raised his face and his fists to the sky, and let out a bellow of rage. It was a long, hoarse, animal scream that might have echoed far— but was lost on the vastness of the sea and sky like a mere whisper.

Impulsively, he tore off his clothes—all but his briefs—and threw himself into the water. He wanted to swim like a shark, attack the problem that was eating him alive, and tear at it with his bare hands. Instead, the warm salty water soothed his rage. Worn out after thrashing aimlessly for some minutes, he all but crawled back to shore and collapsed in exhaustion on the warm sand. Still overcome with emotion, he pounded the sand with his fist. Slowly, he sat up and sat there, letting the sun and wind dry him off. He felt spent and empty.

After a time, a sense of urgency began to gnaw at him. Was his absence creating any more damage? Did he have the right to leave his post like this? Drying sand rasped at him like sandpaper as he pulled his pants on, his shirt, his socks and shoes. He ignored the chafing of his wet skin and underwear, and the rasp of sand against sensitive skin, as he jogged back to Falk's headquarters.

By the time he arrived, a leaden sense of depression had settled on the headquarters. Clerks typed quietly, with dark expressions. Staff officers and NCOs passed in the hall with a gloomy sense of mission, as if they were attending a funeral.

When Jack arrived outside Falk's office, he saw a cluster of NCOs working at a large white board. On the board, they scrawled updates in hurried green and black marker pen. Casualties were listed by numbers, broken down by nationality. Known dead: at this point, 55. Wounded—at least 88. How many U.S., French, British, African? Nobody had sorted that much out as yet.

"Jack."

He turned. Falk stood in his office door, signaling for him to enter.

He found himself alone with the admiral a moment later, with the door locked. "Jack, I was looking for you."

"Sorry, Sir, I was down on the beach having a fit."

"I understand. I need you here now."

"I was trying to figure out if I should blame myself."

"We don't have time for that now," Falk said angrily. "It doesn't matter if you or I or whoever is the biggest fool in the world right now. We have a job to do."

"Of course. Sorry."

"No room for sorry either. Listen—get Rebekah, Don, and Maro together. Pull in anyone else you want. I keep Lew by my side, but you can talk with him. Brief me as needed. What is going to happen next? We have data coming in from all over the world.

We have the attention of the Pentagon, the White House, you name it. I don't think it's hit the press yet. They're still talking about searching the Indian Ocean—China, Japan, Australia, Malaysia, everyone with a boat, a plane, or a paddle is out there canoeing around looking for pieces of the plane. The thing is, Jack, we need to find that plane before it can be used against us and our allies."

"You still think it's in Africa, Sir?"

"Do you?"

"Yes I do." He squared his shoulders. "It seems obvious to me that we are on the same thought track as our enemies. We know who they are—Al Qaeda, Boko Haram, Al Shabaab. Camp Zero was a distraction, but I think we got close to them."

"What do we do, Jack? Tell me, Jack. What do we do?"

"How about this? Let's start over from the beginning. Let's look at every scrap of evidence again. Let's retrace every step. There must be some tiny detail we overlooked."

"Fair enough," Falk said. "There is a two star somebody flying here from Europe to take charge of the operation. I'll be working for them. I'm being superseded here, though I don't know where we are headed with this. I don't care. I just want to get to the truth."

"So do I, Sir."

"Must be frustrating for you, not being in the field."

"Yes—especially not knowing what happened to my men."

"I am so sorry about that."

"I know. Me too." They put a hand, each on the other's shoulder, and squeezed.

"Hang in there," Jack said.

"Yeah," Falk said in a raspy voice.

"I'll set up shop down the hall. You know where to find me."

"I'll be down there banging on your door," Falk promised. "Go on. Get going. Find me something. Save the day."

"No guarantees," Jack said, "but we'll get through this." He thought about Robert and Marian Keaka as he walked down the hall to a barren cubbyhole, his new office, shaking his head and feeling once again stunned.

17.   Andaman Sea Revisited, and a Clue

Jack's new office was next door to the liaison pool, in which Rebekah, Don, and several NATO reps from European nations had desks set up.

The first break came as he and his two friends were sharing tea with Maro, whose office had been moved into the support staff digs around Falk's office.

Falk's liaison Lew Minchao stopped in. "Sign of hope."

"What?" Maro asked, sitting up. Jack, Don, and Rebekah followed suit.

Minchao pulled up a chair and sat on it backwards, kneading the back support with his pale fists. "It's a strange bit of news, but I got confirmation just an hour ago that Thai intelligence have located the area where the plane was refitted."

"Lay it on us," Jack said.

"Myanmar. Burma."

"Wow," said Maro.

"I've been getting information in all morning," Lew said. "Here is what I know so far. As you know, Myanmar or Burma is another of those closed societies run by dictators. They have been run by a military junta for decades, which was replaced by an elected civilian government in recent years, but the abuses continue. That includes child soldiers, sexual slavery, and a whole lot of heavy-handed actions that make them look more like Africa than Asia. They are right next door to our allies in Thailand, who have their own history of corruption and instability, but nothing as bad as Burma. And Thailand stood by the West through the whole Vietnam War ordeal half a century ago, so we have a history together. Anyway, Thailand has been quietly using its own Special Forces on land, air, and sea to probe this idea you came up with, namely about Flight 777 having passed through their back yard. The United States has lent Thailand drone support. By night and by day, we've been going over every inch of the Bay of Bengal. Our Indian allies have been combing through their territories, which includes some wild islands still in the stone ages. Sri Lanka has looked over its territory, and the Burmese have promised to help out as well. Burma is still kind of closed and paranoid, so Thailand and the U.S. have had to help them out a bit." Lew winked. "If you know what I mean."

Maro pressed: "Do we know where Flight 777 set down?"

Lew said: "It seems they landed the plane on a jungle road on the island of Ramree. A stretch of road runs parallel to the shore a little distance inland on the west side of the island near the north end. They needed maybe an hour to fuel up, get rid of the bodies, and fly on toward Africa. You had it right, Jack. All they needed to do was land in the middle of the night on a deserted stretch of road without police patrols. They had about thirty goons waiting. They had already killed all the passengers by depressurizing the cabin a few hours earlier over the Gulf of Thailand. None of the passengers suffered for more than a minute or two. Most were settling down to sleep, so they never knew what hit them."

Jack gritted his teeth as he imagined Robert and Marian in a horrifying environment—the door blown, the cabin whirling with frigid air, a howling sound, maybe some passengers' lungs being forcefully sucked outward into the partial vacuum—then a white haze filling the icy air, and the peace of oblivion.

"The bastards took the plane down to a mile or less as Penang military radar picked up a last trace of them. They flew north along the coast, past Thailand, and set down on a shore road on this island off the coast of Burma. This is the infamous island of Ramree, where hundreds of Japanese soldiers were eaten alive during a night in January 1945 while they were fleeing from the British. It's in the range of these enormous saltwater crocodiles that are the top of the food chain and have no natural enemies except maybe for a human being with a fifty caliber machine gun."

Jack said: "I hate to go over it again, but I think it's all we can do. You say we put drones in there?"

"Yes. We know exactly where their goons were waiting when the plane set down. They unloaded the bodies onto a barge, which they towed a mile south along the shore—to a large estuary, a scary place full of mosquitoes, crocodiles, snakes, you name it."

Maro injected: "But no people live near there?"

"Not really," Minchao said. "That is the insane little beauty of the plan. There are a few villagers on the island, and a few miles of road. It's a huge island, about fifty miles long parallel to the mainland, and about twenty miles wide on average. The enemy threw all 241 bodies into an empty barge and used the oil tanker, after they filled the jet's fuel tanks, to tow the barge down to the estuary. They towed it a quarter mile inland, opened the petcocks, and left it low in the water line for the crocodiles to climb on board and feast. We've spotted the barge. Then they took the fuel tanker out to sea and probably just parked it wherever they stole it. They used an unmotorized barge to avoid leaving an oil slick if they sank it. However, they weren't counting on a big rust slick that one of our orbiting satellites picked up on the water."

"Maybe on purpose," Don said. "More sardonic jokes to poke their finger in our eye."

"Visible from space," Jack echoed. "NSA has been busy."

"Of course. With a fine toothed comb," Minchao said.

"Makes sense," Rebekah chimed in.

"The rest is as you said, Jack. They didn't bother repainting the fuselage—the fisherman in the Maldives says he saw the red markings on a white background of Malaysia Air. Also, it was flying low, meaning they did not take time to fix or replace the door they blew. They couldn't get back up to altitude."

"It's a waste of Jet-A flying low," Don said. "But evidently they could afford to waste the fuel in the thick atmosphere. The fisherman said the noise was deafening, which makes sense in the thick, moist atmosphere just above sea level."

Jack snapped his fingers. "I have a question. Did they find any evidence of netting?"

Minchao looked baffled.

Jack explained: "At Camp Zero, they had spread a purposely false color camouflage cover so our satellites would notice. The question is—did they pick this up on Ramree, or did they have it waiting in Africa? It's a slim lead if anything."

"What are you thinking, Jack?" asked Don.

"I am wondering if they have another set of netting—the real camouflage. Either the plane is inside a hangar someplace in Africa right now, or else it is in a setup similar to Camp Zero but for real—with effective camouflage over it. The real thing, with colors that match the terrain. If by some chance they had the real netting sitting there on that tanker, let's say, and loaded it onto the plane, and if we could get a few square inches of it, we might be able to figure out if they are hiding the plane in grassland, desert, mountains, or who knows what."

"Actually," Minchao said, "the Thai commandos who went in picked up some artifacts. They photographed the blown door, which they found lying half submerged in a drainage canal by the road. They picked up shreds of clothing from the deceased passengers, including some children's toys, ladies' purses, that sort of thing. Maybe they did pick up some camouflage material. We can ask."

"Whom do we speak with?" Jack asked.

"I have a counterpart in Bangkok who is liaison with the Thai navy. Their divers and special forces actually went in after the drones located the site. If anyone saw anything, it would be their commando teams."

"Can we get them on an uplink?"

"I can set it up, Jack. Give me a little while."

Minchao was true to his word.

Jack waited with his companions in a dusky room filled with servers and other computer equipment. On the monitor was the face of a Thai navy commander, speaking from a base in Yangon (Rangoon), a short distance inland from the Gulf of Martaban. "Good evening," said Cdr. Thamrong Boonsong. He was a pleasantly competent looking man, prematurely bald, with gold-rimmed glasses. He wore an olive-green flight suit with brightly colored insignia of rank and unit. "What can I do to help you?"

Jack explained his search for evidence of camouflage material.

"My men found evidence that pile of military-style material had been stored by one side of the road," Boonsong said. "It had evidently been dragged in off the barge that we told your people about. All of this was well coordinated ahead of time."

"If you could fax me the exact color scheme of that material," Jack said, "I would be grateful."

Boonsong shrugged. "Not a problem, Captain. We have already digitized it through our forensic evidence facility. We are treating this as a criminal case because of the connection with the missing airliner. All hush-hush and top secret, of course. I'll have that information emailed to you while we are still talking."

Sure enough, within fifteen minutes, a technician sitting near Jack exclaimed. An email had arrived from Thailand with an attachment—a jpeg file containing a swatch of colors.

Jack thanked the Thai officer and rang off. He waited as a computer tech used a graphics processing application to examine the file. Shortly, the technician printed out an array of RGB values representing the colors on the swatch of torn cloth that had been left behind in the dirt on Ramree Island. It was unmistakably debris from camouflage netting. To Jack's rather sickened delight, the image in the graphics package did not resemble the russet and yellow fall colors of the dome at Camp Zero. "We are in luck," he said. "It's not a match. That means we now have a color match on the general area where they have Flight 777. And that, my friends, is desert camo. Having been to Afghanistan and other points in the region, I recognize it without batting an eyelash."

Don squinted skeptically at the image on the screen. It looked like a bunch of light cocoa scratches on a clay-colored background. "That could be anywhere from Algeria to the Indus Valley. Good luck, Jack."

"I know, we are trawling desperately," Jack said. "But look, it does narrow things down a bit. We can assume they have the plane in Africa—almost certainly in the northern tier. We can tell NSA and whoever else has satellites to stop looking at jungles and savannahs." He rose. "I'm going to see Falk. He'll be glad we have a straw to clutch at."

As Jack walked into the main office pod on the second deck, where Falk had his headquarters, he was startled to see the offices and the hallway leading to them crowded with rear ends—uniformed and otherwise. Men and women, they were intent on a large screen hanging from a ceiling corner in the master chief petty officer's quarters. Displayed on the screen were images from the mission in Africa gone horribly wrong.

"You've got to be kidding me," Jack said out loud as he started to press through the crowd.

"No seriously," a woman said, "it's breaking news. It's being watched all over the world."

Someone else said: "Looks really bad."

"They got themselves a propaganda victory."

On television, the announcer's voice overrode repetitively playing images, which was probably all the media had at this moment: a charred body sprawled over a hummock of earth; a splintered palm tree with a broken chopper blade embedded in it, a hospital chopper with a big red cross on a white field, hovering over a black, flattened circle in otherwise heavy green vegetation, and a squad of African soldiers in green uniforms, lugging ammo boxes down a jungle trail.

Jack made his way to the master chief NCO's desk, which was deserted at the moment. Jack wondered if the woman had barricaded herself in Falk's office. He pressed ahead and knocked on the door leading to the inner suite. Getting no answer, he pushed into the inner lobby. There, more men and women sat around a television set. The doors in the circular wall were open, revealing similar scenes in the offices themselves.

"Dorsey," Falk said when Jack finally reached him. The admiral and his top staff and advisers were clustered around a television set as well. "Come on in. Ain't this grand?"

Jack stepped in just as the female master chief petty officer turned the TV off. "It's the same stuff over and over again," she said.

The announcer's voice floated across the air among all the televisions and computer monitors: "Al Jazeera announced this morning that they had received an anonymous tip about a top secret, critical U.S.-European combined military operation in Africa that has gone horribly wrong. The independent Arabic network did not specify who leaked the story to them, but speculation is rife that one of the octopus tentacles of Al Qaeda in the Middle East was responsible. According to Al Jazeera's source, Western military units were lured into an ambush in the Central African Republic overnight. Western units, including elements of the French Foreign Legion, British Special Air Services, and United States Special Forces, were on a mission to recover what they thought to be the Malaysian airliner that has been missing for over six weeks. Jubilant crowds can be seen dancing in the streets of the Palestinian territories, Tehran, Mogadishu, and other radicalized Islamic communities. Our affiliates in the region confirm that millions of West-hating ordinary civilians have been whipped into a frenzy…"

Falk told his staff: "Please give me a minute alone with Captain Dorsey." Moments later, he threw himself back in his desk chair and motioned for Jack to take one of the seats facing him. The others had cleared from the room.

Jack said: "Here I was, thinking I had good news for you."

Falk laid his forehead onto his palms, and shook his head like a wet dog shaking off water. "Hit me, brother. I need it."

Jack held up the computer printouts. "We have some evidence from the Andaman Sea site. Did you know that our side found out where the plane landed?"

Falk looked up with a red-rimmed face. "Minchao briefly told me before pandemonium broke loose here in my offices."

Jack said: "It's not much, but it's an indication that they brought in some desert cover for the plane." He explained that Thai commandos had found a place along the roadside on Ramree where stacks of folded camo netting had been stored. "We got some scraps, which went to a military forensics lab in Bangkok, and they came up with a profile."

"Which is?"

"Libya, possibly. The great sand desert that spans the corner where Egypt, Libya, Chad, and northern Sudan run together. This was actually one of my candidate areas before the Equatorial jungles came into play."

Falk tapped a pencil on this desk. "So you think that our enemies are done playing games?"

"They still have options, Sir, but I think they have played most of their deck."

Falk carried the metaphor forward: "But have they played all their aces? Is there still anything big coming?"

"We have to assume the absolute worst," Jack said. "They stole a passenger liner. They pulled this stunt in C.A.R. I don't think the Camp Zero ambush was the key reason for hijacking Flight 777."

"You're right. We have to assume they've got us on the run."

"They released the story to Al Jazeera to score propaganda points. Until we have the actual plane, let's assume there is more."

"I agree," Falk said. "I was on the phone with Stuttgart already, and they have talked with Washington. Two can play this game. We all agree that the best thing we can do now is to come out with a press release, even if we have been trumped."

"What do you think, Sir?"

Falk sat with his hands folded together, coiled like a mass of wire and muscle. Jack felt for him. The man was obviously an athlete and a boots on the ground sort of guy. Or wings in the air. This desk jockeying was not his cup of tea, but his rank and grade demanded it. "We can trump them at their own game, Jack."

"Are you thinking what I am thinking, Sir?"

Falk grinned. "Great minds think alike. Yeah, probably. We do the best thing now that is left to us, which is to play dumb."

"I like it. I hate it, but I like it."

"We let them think they fooled us. They made fools of us, okay, and we lost a lot of good people."

"I'm waiting for word on my team, Sir."

"I know. The Chief is out there, making calls. Sometimes we get lost in our own secrecy. It's sensitive stuff—gotta make sure the families don't find out before we can send the black car with the two officers to their house."

Jack thought of Robert and Marian Keaka, of Ben Latoni and Ray Marston, of Greg Boileau and Shep Sepak, and the rest of the A and B Teams he had sent in harm's way. His gut felt in a twist.

"The show has to go on, Jack—for their sake as well as ours."

"I know, Sir. I'm with you."

Falk pointed to the muted computer monitor. "We can't stop the media from playing that footage over and over again. We can feed in some misinformation of our own. By the time in 2011 that we got into that compound in Abbottabad and shot Osama bin Laden dead, despite whoever was protecting him locally, we got pretty good at this cat walking. You know what cat walking is?"

"I'm afraid to ask."

"You know that cats in a neighborhood don't have any regard for fences and other human barriers. They have their own sense of territory. When you see a cat walking around, he's not just out for a walk. Cats do not just stroll around. If you see a cat walking by your house, that cat is on a mission. He is about to help the dogs or cats next door eat their lunch. That's how this war has gotten to be. There are no fences and no gates. We just walk in wherever we need to and help these dirtballs eat their lunch. We eat their lunch for them. We eat them along with their lunch."

"Right, Sir."

"Speaking of lunch, I am waiting for a call from Naples."

"Ah, Italy. You order some pizza, Sir?"

"Yeah right. Our command structure has been ghosted to a two-star fireball in Naples, who is going to be running the Africa show from here on, independent of Stuttgart and anyone else we know. I'm waiting to hear from our new boss as we speak. We're going to have a new operational handle as well. I imagine it means they'll be throwing the Sixth Fleet at the problem now. Army and Air Force will hand over the powder. Navy wants to run with the ball and shine. And of course the Marines have been in it from the start."

"I could use a stiff drink," Jack said, rising and looking at the counter to his right, "but some black coffee will have to do."

"It's in the carafe. Can you make that two?"

"Will do."

As Jack poured two cups of steaming black coffee—which had an aroma akin to a tire factory on a hot summer day—he heard a sound and turned, just to see the ceiling monitor flicker on.

"That must be my Chief, sending the call through," Falk said. He and Jack hunkered around Falk's desk, nursing their cups, as technicians sorted out the signals.

A woman's face filled the screen. "Admiral Falk?"

"Yes, Ma'am. Paul Falk, and with me is one of my field commanders, Captain (acting Major) Jack Dorsey."

"Gentlemen," said the stern African-American visage. "I am Rear Admiral Janice Taylor. Effective today, I am commanding admiral of this operation, and your new commanding officer. Let's speak alone for a few minutes, Admiral Falk."

"Yes Ma'am." Falk signaled for Jack to vacate but stay in the area. Jack picked up his coffee, and quietly let himself out of the room. Only after he had clicked the door shut did he hear the conversation in the room pick up again—her voice in the lead.

Jack found that the Chief Master Petty Officer, a forty-something blonde woman with glasses named Lorraine Dischler, had cleared the offices and restored order. All but one of the displays had been turned off, and the CNN coverage continued to roll with the same tired pictures.

"The Old Man getting the riot act read?" Dischler asked as she sat at her desk, dusting photos and reestablishing order in her domain—and Falk's.

"It's all politics," Jack told her. "You know how it is. Falk is a good officer and they'll keep him in a good place."

"Where Falk goes, so I go," Dischler said. "It's been good the past six years."

"You made rank in this job?"

She nodded, glancing fondly across photos of her family, and at the wall photo of Admiral Falk, as well as the Secretary of the Navy, and the President of the United States. "I'll be eligible to retire in another two years. I'll stay on if Admiral Falk wants me." She grinned at him. "When are you going to make Admiral, Sir?"

He set his cup down, took a chair, and put his feet up. "We don't have admirals in the Army, Chief. You wouldn't know that."

She grinned, opening her drawer and sorting through the office supplies there. Jack noticed a nice fat 9 mm Glock strapped into a worn leather holster. "You're a civilian, huh?" she said.

"Reserve. I'll soon be teaching History at a nice university, if I get through this situation with my head still attached."

"That's nice," she said in a warm, chatty tone. "My husband is CEO of an electronics company. Interesting work."

"Kids?"

"A daughter, sixteen, in private school in Boston."

"She must be your everything."

"I fly there every chance I can."

"We'll try to get you to Boston as soon as possible," Jack said. "Need to get this mess over with. In answer to your question, I'd like to stay at captain or major for the rest of my career with Uncle Sam. It's less paperwork and more fun."

She flashed an admiring look. "Field guy, huh? Man of action."

At that moment, a female technician in Navy camo poked her blonde head in. "Mandatory broadcast in two minutes, Chief."

"Put it on," Dischler instructed.

The young women, in her late teens and serious beyond her years, strode into the room. She had the unisex look—lean, boyish, a bit delicate—as so many young women poured into that mold, complete with black combat boots and, stuck in her back pocket like a farmer's handkerchief, a utility cap. The yeoman turned on the television monitor and waited as an image floated into view.

The image was from the White House. It was of a podium with the Presidential seal on its front, a hallway stretching away behind it, and flags on either side. Far away in the capital, a young man in a business suit stepped into the frame of vision and made some adjustments on the podium surface, out of sight. A hand came out of nowhere and placed a water carafe out of sight but within reach of those about to speak.

The camera scanned the room, showing a packed audience of news crews and field reporters.

The camera swiveled back as a voice said: "Ladies and gentlemen, the President of the United States."

Without formalities, the President and two other dignitaries stepped up. "I won't keep you long because we all have work to do," said the President. "I will keep my remarks brief because today's show belongs to the Secretary of State. We are doing this in the White House rather than at State to underscore this Administration's complete support for our uniformed services across the country and around the world, as well as the thousands of dedicated civilians of the Foreign Service and other civilian organizations who serve us every day and so admirably. As you have heard from certain foreign news organizations, we and our allies met with a deadly incident involving our enemies—yesterday, by today's Washington calendar. I just want to remind you that the path to victory is never easy, but crossed with disappointments and bitter losses. We and our allies have lost a significant number of heroic service members in the Central African Republic, for whom we grieve. We are in the process of gathering the facts in the field, and preparing to notify the families of those affected. I would have preferred not to speak prematurely of this, but our enemies have shown the bad taste and lack of human sensitivity to publicly celebrate their ongoing campaign of murder and assassination. I want to emphasize once again that we—from my office on down through the hierarchy—are standing firm, we stand together, and we shall in the end be victorious. Our cause is just, our means are appropriate, our warriors are courageous, and our units are prepared. I now turn the podium over to our Secretary of State."

The Secretary of State, a woman, stepped to the podium while the President stepped aside. She was accompanied by the Chairman of the Joint Chiefs of Staff, a tall, grizzled Air Force General whose dark blue uniform was laden with medals, citations, and other decorations. She said: "Thank you, Mr. President. Just under 24 hours ago, our forces in central Africa launched a combined assault on a position known as Camp Zero. Participating were U.S., French, British, Kenyan, and other regional national units. These were adequately and properly supported by a professional, logistical supply line stretching hundreds or thousands of miles to rear bases and to the various homelands of the combatants. Despite the best intelligence from satellites and local ranger and pathfinder units, it appears that we were lured into an ambush that resulted in several dozen casualties on our side."

As she spoke, a hubbub of voices grew in the room. She spoke in a measured tone and manner, pausing between sentences to look up and cast her steady gaze around the room in a show of strength and control. "The action at Camp Zero resulted in our seizing of the position and the area around it, but the enemy had fled. The grounds were booby trapped with explosives, causing a number of allied combat troops to be wounded or lose their lives. Our forces were able to administer first aid on the scene, while securing the area. Our forces were able to bring up immediate medical teams and evacuation resources, so that at this time no wounded troops are left in theater and no deceased service members are unaccounted for. The President and I feel, as does the Chairman, that our best recourse is total honesty and open disclosure at this time to dispel as much of the naturally occurring rumor machinery as possible. In the decades since the West has been under attack from these assailants, we have acquitted ourselves well and maintained the upper hand. We have lost no ground. No nation has fallen to them. If anything, the West has gained allies and supporters. We maintain a clear and realistic vision that this is a real war, with bloody battles and real casualties, and we have shed a painful amount of valuable blood and treasure in the cause of liberty and progress..."

Jack and Dischler watched as the speeches continued. They were followed by open mike questions, which the dignitaries fielded—often pointed and harassing, even sometimes borderline political, but always kept on target by a White House assistant press secretary with masterful control of the room.

The door opened, and Falk stuck his head out. "Dorsey?"

Jack popped to his feet and approached the boss. Dischler hurried behind him, ready to help her boss as well.

"Both of you, come in," Falk said.

Jack and MCPO Dischler took seats. Falk closed the door and strode to his chair, behind the desk and before the window. "Lew Minchao is across the island, as is Maro, so I'll brief them later. We have our marching orders. We are now part of Operation Iron Bulwark, run from U.S. Naval Headquarters in Naples. I have no idea who picked that name or why. I remain your field commander on Diego Garcia. The difference is that we now have top level visibility—but it's shifted to NATO, in Europe, meaning that we can continue to do our little thing here with Operation Lima, but under the new operational handle OIB. Lima Triple died with those people at Camp Zero. I have some really bad news, Jack."

Jack felt his face turning pale, blood draining, as Falk read off the names of dead and wounded from Team A. "Ben Latoni, evacuated to Nairobi, comatose, in critical condition. Ray Marston, deceased. Shep Sepak, deceased." He read off a few more names, all wounded who were expected to live. Jack took the news with trembling hands, sitting down. Images of Ray and Shep passed through his memories, as did Ben Latoni's.

Falk said: "I'm sorry, Jack. I know they were personal friends of yours. I'm so sorry." He added: "They did what they were supposed to do. They took the high ground, in more ways than one. They held their position at Camp Zero, exchanging intelligence with the French and British commanders as they tightened their advance on the presumed aircraft under the netting. When the first round of explosions went off, Ray took shrapnel and died instantly. I have a full accounting of the last moments from Greg Boileau, who was on the heights with them. Greg had just turned and bent over to pull up an ammo box when the first explosion went off. He turned and started toward Marston's position, when Shep said something to him. At that moment, Ben Latoni made a cell call to you."

"I got it," Jack said in a shaky voice. "He was able to say my name, basically, and then he was cut off. I had no idea what was going down."

"Apparently, the second set of explosions went off a minute or two later, all over the area, killing Shep, who had stood up for a moment. Damn devils, they must have spent a lot of time and imagination planning how their charges would go off, after their fighters hightailed it into the bush."

"Have we caught any of them?"

Falk shook his head. "Nope. They were long gone—about fifty or more—a mixed sack of Chechens, Malaysians, and other international Islamic fundamentalists. I'm sure some corrupt local officials in C.A.R. got paid off. Maybe the fighters flew out under cover of darkness after the pathfinders thought they had secured the area. They are gone. Jack, we have to get real focused and stay focused. Our job is to find that aircraft before they can pull off something far more spectacular."

"What do you think?" Jack said.

"You're the one with the imagination," Falk said. "What is your guess?"

Jack hesitated. "I don't even want to say it."

"Please do," Dischler urged.

"Get it on the table," Falk said.

Jack told them: "At a guess, if I wanted to really upstage what they did on 9/11, I'd kill more people and do it in a more spectacular manner. Not only that, but 9/11 was one of those medium is the message deals—the Twin Towers of the World Trade Center were a symbol of global Western commerce. There were also false stories that they were controlled by the usual Zionist bankers, full of Jews, all that music to the ears of haters. Even U.S.-based haters picked up on that in the years after 9/11."

Dischler said: "What would be an even bigger, juicier target?"

Falk added: "What would get those people in Gaza and Tehran dancing up and down in the streets again?"

Jack spoke hesitantly: "How about a strike on the Vatican? Saint Peter's Basilica during High Mass on a Sunday? Or how about Saint Paul's Cathedral in London, during a High Mass on a Sunday, only it's the Anglicans rather than the Catholics?"

"No Eastern Orthodox?" Falk asked with grim humor.

Jack put on his History professor hat. "The Orthodox were put out of commission when the Ottomans conquered Constantinople in 1453. They took another hit in 1917 when the Russian revolution put the Romanovs out of business. Stalin did them no favors in Moscow. And, as to more visible, modern Protestants, one logical hit would be on the National Cathedral in Washington, D.C.— which however is (a) too far to reach without being detected and refueling and (b) just a continuation of the Saint Paul scenario in

London. I should mention that they'd probably enjoy knocking the Eiffel Tower down. Those are about the most spectacular targets I can think of."

"Very scary," Dischler said.

"We have no time to lose," Falk said. "Put that scenario together, Jack. Meanwhile, I will coordinate with NSA and the other agencies to follow up your lead on the desert camo. Talk to Rebekah and Don."

"I am talking with them," Jack said. "They have Israel and Hormuz under control. Also, as much as some of the Islamic factions hate each other, I cannot imagine a hit on Mecca or Medina. I'd rule that out."

"Whatever they have planned," Jack said, "it will be revenge for the killing of bin Laden. And it will be a spectacular attack on the West—most likely of a religious nature against those they consider to be Crusaders, or followers of the Cross of Christendom. The more brazen and horrifying their crimes, the more support they will stir up among the poorest and most ignorant people in the Islamic world. They need a showy victory, and the next strike will be it. We need to figure out what it is, and stop them."

Falk said: "Whatever the outcome turns out to be with Flight 777, there will be more to follow. Even if we defeat them on this missing airliner gambit, they still win among the lowest of the low among their followers because they challenge the West. They ignore their dictators, and see us as the source of all their problems, especially Israel."

Jack added: "The sad thing is that few of them know their history. The Islamic assault on the Christian world began in the 7th Century. During the Plague of Justinian, entire North African cities died out. The Islamic armies swept across North Africa from the Arabian Peninsula to Morocco virtually unopposed. The Byzantines lost North Africa, and never recouped it. The Byzantines did conquer back the Holy Land area, which they softened up for the Crusaders who came later, but they Europe was driven out of the Middle East until the 20th Century.

"The Arabs and Berbers under Islam invaded the Iberian Peninsula, cross the Pyrenees Mountains, and invaded what is now France in the 8th Century, until they were stopped by Charles (called the Hammer) Martel at Poitiers in 732. They had already conquered Spain by then, which they held until the last Moors were driven out of Grenada in 1492. Muslim armies invaded Italy, conquering Sicily and Bari in the 800s, and tried to conquer France by going north through there. And again they conquered part of Europe in the 1400s under the Ottomans, which they continue to hold today. In fact, the last major Islamic military invasion of Europe stopped short of the gates of Vienna just before 1600. Not that the West was much to brag about in many ways, but we should all bury our hatchets and live happily ever after. The common people of the world deserve it, once the agitators and dictators are done telling their lies, and stirring up war and death. We need to learn from history, so we don't repeat the mistakes of the past."

Part Four: Finale—Cliff-Hanger

19.   More Scenarios— Cities of Europe (3).

Jack Dorsey set up his new operation in a large office suite down the hall from Admiral Falk. Although Lew Minchao, Rebekah Goldstein, and Don Malik (as he styled himself in a Westernized mode, complete with cowboy hat and Nashville drawl) had their own offices elsewhere, Jack requisitioned desks for them. He also had several guest spaces brought in, including one for Maro. He had Filipino work crews arrange the desks in a row against one wall. In the center of the room, under overly bright fluorescent lights, he had his long table brought up from the hangar. He was glad to be out of there, since he couldn't bear working there amid the ghosts of Ben Latoni and Ray Marston. By now, Ray's and Shep's remains had been repatriated to Dover Air Force Base in Maryland for ceremonies and processing to their home towns and families. Ben Latoni was still in guarded condition, but recovering slowly from a head wound at the Defense Department's Landstuhl Regional Medical Center in Germany, just a short drive from NATO Air Forces Headquarters at Ramstein Air Force Base. Ben was still not able to talk coherently on the phone. Jack tried calling the Medium Care Unit at Landstuhl, and spoke with Ben's wife Shelley, whom he had last seen under pleasant circumstances on the beaches of Malaysia. Jack also had a tearful conversation with Latrice Marston at her home in St. Louis, Missouri.

FNE workers brought up Jack's table and maps, and his monitors hung from the ceiling as they had earlier. For the moment, he was betwixt and between. He did not have a field assignment— his troops had gone with Shep Sepak and Greg Boileau. Greg Boileau and the members of Team A had been removed to Naples, where they were subject to intense debriefing with ONI, Military Intelligence, CIA, and other intelligence agencies.

Jack, Maro, and Minchao processed much of the traffic coming in to Falk's headquarters now, with Minchao as Chief of Staff and Maro as Adjutant General. Minchao fed relevant bits to Jack, while Maro was still Jack's nominal boss. Maro had a capable assistant A.G., a Navy officer named Peter Boyle, a young Afro-American ROTC officer from Rochester Polytechnic with ambitions in the engineering field. With Boyle handling day to day administrative duties, Maro was free to concentrate on special projects—and

Jack's was one of these. Jack briefly considered, and quickly dismissed, the idea of asking for evacuation back to San Diego as Catherine's term drew near. Maro had the orders and other paperwork standing by in a desk drawer, along with standby flight priority. With that handled, Jack felt he should concentrate on the next leg of this Flight 777 mystery story.

Jack met with Don and Rebekah privately, while Maro sat in.

Rebekah—her eyes more soulfully large than ever—said: "I have told you before. I think they are going to strike very soon. They know they are getting stale on the ground."

Don agreed. "They will strike very soon. It's only a matter of time before the world's intelligence organizations and satellite reconnaissance capabilities find the aircraft. Will we be in time?"

"They hid it well," Jack said. "We still don't have a clue where. What about the desert swatches?"

Maro said: "I got the analysis back from Langley, which has our liaison point with NSA and the rest of the alphabet soup. CIA's best guess is that the netting is suitable for the desert between Egypt, Libya, Chad, and Sudan. That covers an area about the size of Europe, I am afraid. It's filled with desert, mountains, dunes as big as seven story buildings—let me put it this way, more hiding places than the Taliban had in the wilderness of Afghanistan."

"Wonderful," Jack said. "I love a challenge."

Later in the day, he met with Don in Don's office on the third floor. The Saudi liaison for Lima Triple and similar projects consisted of a Saudi Air Force Colonel (Don) along with a Saudi technical sergeant trained to handle their own encrypted messages and to assist Don. On the first floor of the building, the Israelis had a similar section, headed by Rebekah Goldstein and two attractive young female IDF staffers, one a lieutenant, the other a sergeant. Elsewhere in the building, a new suite of offices was building assembled by the ubiquitous FNE for a European Union coordination office of the Rapid Deployment Force. Now that the focus of interest for Flight 777 had expanded beyond Africa, the EU and NATO were putting resources on the ground at Diego Garcia and elsewhere.

Don had with him a young Saudi, whom he introduced as Captain Mohammed bin Abdullah of the Royal Saudi Air Force. Amid pleasantries, Abdullah told Jack: "My government has made a special project of examining our own desert areas, most notably Rub' al Khali or the Empty Quarter, where this missing aircraft could be stationed. It may be unlikely, but we would be remiss not to take into account the possibility that our enemies would made a strike on Mecca and thus outrage the entire Islamic world against my government. I am happy to report that we have found no evidence of Flight 777 on our territory, and our allies around the Emirates report similar results. Egypt, in particular, is scouring the Sinai Peninsula for points of opportunity. I think we have all the bases covered, Jack."

"I'm happy to hear that," Jack told him. "So I can assume that your forces will patrol and keep an eye out in case this aircraft suddenly rises from a sand dune?"

Abdullah, who had a wide face, friendly eyes, and a full mustache, smiled broadly. "I can promise you that and more. We are coordinating with the Israelis, the Egyptians, and the Emirates to ensure that nothing gets airborne unless we allow it. The skies in our region are already militarized, but now also on a red alert."

Later, meeting with Don and Rebekah, Jack told them of his puzzlement: "What can the crazies be planning?"

"I have told you before," Rebekah said. "Israel thinks that the window of opportunity for these terrorists is closing fast. As they lose the element of surprise, it's only a matter of time before the missing 777 is found."

"Yes," Don said, "and of course it will come as no surprise that we have several countries lined up with commando teams to seize the plane the minute anyone sees it. Turkey has a military unit ready. Saudi Arabia and Kuwait have teams ready. Egypt has a special forces brigade on standby."

"Israel has missile squadrons waiting," Rebekah said.

"As do all the Arab allies," Don seconded. "Which makes it all the more puzzling. They must have thought ahead through all this."

Jack continued to study maps spread out across the long table, under the idly churning images of news and weather on the hanging monitors. Using a work station at his desk, Jack plunged into research on public Internet sites. Keeping busy kept him from losing his mind. He was running out of options, and he did not have an intelligence staff to back him up with grunt work. He was striking out on his own. He was in Admiral Falk's back pocket as an emergency spare—a role he agreed was needed.

He divided his time into two activities. On the one side, with the cooperation of Minchao and others on Falk's staff, he started assembling a shadow strike force to replace his lost Special Forces unit. At Minchao's somewhat sentimental suggestion, they designated it Team C. The field unit was, at this point, little more than a roomful of backpacks, weapons, and other supplies kept under lock and key down the hall from Jack's office.

Jack spent the rest of his time on a new focus. He picked several European cities—Rome, London, Paris, and Berlin, and began tracing back the times and logistics required for the hijacked Flight 777 to theoretically leave a North African hiding place. Using Khartoum, Sudan as a hypothetical, stand-in point of origin, he calculated the flight times on a direct line to be rather short for a fully fueled, mostly empty Boeing 777 traveling at over 500 m.p.h. cruising speed at 35,000 feet operational altitude.

For argument's sake, Cairo meant about 1,000 miles or two hours' flight time at 500 miles or 800 kilometers per hour.

From Khartoum, a flight to Israel, or Jordan, or for that matter Hormuz could be effected in under 1200 miles, or two and a half hours. To Rome, the distance was about 2,200 miles or 3,500 km— not quite five hours. To Paris, an air flight would take about 2,900 miles or 4,600 km, to be flown in about six hours. London would cover about 3,100 miles or 5,000 km, doable in just over six hours.

The really puzzling aspect was that, if any of these was to be the target, how did the terrorists expect to evade radar networks that had been designed to foil the entire Warsaw Pact cutting edge forces of not long ago? Something was out of round here, but what?

Jack made a list of all locations in Europe that had world-wide notoriety as Western hot spots that on-hangers in the Third World would love to see crippled by sneak attacks—the more spectacular and deadly, the more dancing on dusty streets by individuals who had nothing, and who must blame their miserable existences on anyone other than their own native-born tormentors like Assad, Ghadafi, or Saddam.

Admiral Falk called Jack to his office that afternoon to introduce to him a half dozen NATO and EU Rapid Deployment Strike Force officers. They included lieutenant colonel or major types, accompanied by their top NCOs, from Spain, Italy, Germany, Netherlands, and Poland. More were on the way, covering many of Europe's nations—among them France, Denmark, and Belgium.

The mostly male newcomers were polite, of good cheer, and radiated both competence and self-confidence. Falk's enlisted staff served coffee and pastries in the main lounge of his offices while Falk made a brief, cheery speech.

An Austrian major made a comment Jack most appreciated: "We want to know more about Camp Zero and the missing airliner. The news is out, so we have little to hide. We are here under cover of a major NATO RDF exercise—which does us good anyway."

The men toasted solemnly with their coffees.

A German Luftwaffe major, speaking in flawless English, posed the question: "Gentlemen, while we celebrate here, are we forgetting something?"

They all looked at him.

"A World Cup playoff game is scheduled for today in Paris."

A hubbub of voices rose. By football, he meant what U.S. people would call soccer.

Someone said: "Who is playing?"

Someone else answered: "Morocco versus Ireland."

The German raised his hand again, and silence descended. "Gentlemen, there we have a major target of opportunity. Consider what would happen either way. Morocco, a predominantly Muslim nation, wins—bam, a weaponized airliner slams into central Paris, taking out the Notre Dame Cathedral or the Eiffel Tower, maybe the Arc de Triomphe. Ireland wins—hit the hated Crusaders. It's win-win for the terrorists."

"Yes—but they still have to fly through the radars" said another officer. "Unless they now have invented a magic shield."

Jack felt a mixture of revulsion, fear, and anger. Was there any hope with the primitive hatred in the world today? Jack felt a sense of rage at the meaninglessness. Did humans never learn anything?

The German was right. The soccer match might attract a million fans to Paris, and it would certainly have a billion viewers around the world. The game was a key final turning point. Sports should equalize the playing field between wealthy and poor nations, setting all religions and ethnic groups on an equal footing. The poorest nation in Africa or South America could inflict a stinging and humiliating defeat upon the world's top economic and military powers. It should be a source of pride on the street, not of blood lust. But the human spirit had a dark side, readily evoked by the Saddams and the Milosevics of history.

The Europeans turned to Jack. "Captain, what do you think?"

Jack set his coffee down. "Gentlemen, we have work to do, starting with Paris. Let's look at all possible sensational locations where our enemies may strike. I have run out of ideas."

Falk mentioned as they trooped out to Jack's roost: "Jack, just so you know, Sixth Fleet is going on high alert, moving more ships into the Mediterranean."

"Thanks, Sir," Jack said as he led his new charges down to the map room. Something triggered an alarm deep inside his mind. With all this going on, he was not quite aware of the red flag yet that was going up in the back of his thoughts. A young woman would unexpectedly trigger an epiphany for him—soon—because, as Rebekah kept saying, that airliner was growing stale and needed to be served up while its shock and awe were still fresh.

20.　More Scenarios—Disease Vector (4).

Rebekah and Don introduced themselves to the European officers. Lew Minchao and Maro hovered in the background, while Admiral Falk briefly looked in. Falk briefly caught Jack's eye, gave him an approving nod, and took off with Minchao at his heels. Stuttgart was calling, or maybe it was Langley or the Pentagon or some other high echelon amid the layers of concern and tangle of command structures.

FNE housekeeping staff in brown jumpsuits brought in a small van load of chairs, and the European officers and NCOs soon had seating. Jack's small space was looking very crowded, and he considered moving back to the hangar near the mess hall.

Maro introduce a U.S. Army medical doctor who had been flown in from the United States for the occasion. He was a fifty something, white-haired man, slightly stocky, wearing an ill-fitting brown suit, mustard-yellow leather shoes, and an open-collared white shirt that looked as if he had slept in it on his long flight to Diego Garcia. His hair looked mussy, and he had bags under his eyes. But Dr. Sam Levin's eyes were gray and sharp. "I have been invited to join your activity here because of my specialization in infectious diseases," Levin said. He stood in the limelight amid a semi-circle of seated officers and NCOs. "You are looking at the idea of a city center being hit by this missing aircraft, which seems like a spectacular scenario. I will be coordinating the collection of data on the possibility that the plane will be further weaponized with deadly nuclear, biological, or chemical vectors—anthrax, maybe a genetically altered strain of avian flu, or perhaps some kind of aerosol plague. Now you have an idea of what my colleagues have been doing in places like the U.S. Army Medical Research Institute of Infectious Diseases (USAMRIID) at Fort Detrick, Maryland. We keep our work low key because of the justifiable fear and sometimes the conspiracy paranoia surrounding our activities. Whenever I talk about this, on a rare occasion when I speak behind closed doors to a secure audience like this, I always begin by assuring your that our endeavors are 100% defensive in nature. Sometimes you have to build it to see how it can be used against you. I am here today as part of an effort to make sure no city is struck by a weaponized plane that will spread disease to millions of souls.

"Admittedly, on the one hand, our adversary is looking for propaganda. The more newsworthy their attack, which we have to assume is coming at any moment, the more they will benefit from their intended audience—the already victimized people of the Third World. At the same time, I have to tell you that it would be a waste of resources to load a plane full of delicate disease germs. It would be far more effective to carry them secretly to a U.S. or European location by truck or train. From there, you infect a few dozen or hundred willing, fanatical volunteers. You put them on buses and trains, and drive them into major cities. You give them each a few hundred dollars or Euros, and tell them to have a good time for a few days. By the time they start dropping dead in the gutters, in cheap hotels, in parks, or in restaurants over their last meal—it will be too late. Thousands or millions will have been exposed to disease, and the authorities will of course be unprepared. That is far more efficient than flying the fragile germs in and crashing them in a ball of flame at high energies.

"However, that said, I have been instructed to coordinate a search for any possible signs of biological or similar warfare."

As he spoke, a U.S. Navy petty officer in fatigue uniform hurried in and handed him a note. "Thank you," Levin said. He looked up. "Our network across Africa is already at work. This is a notification through French and Belgian diplomatic channels that UNAFOR, a united command of eastern African nations, has intelligence sources tracking a shipment of a modified Ebola virus that just crossed the Republic of Congo headed eastward. I have no more information than that, but I expect to keep you updated. Apparently, Tanzanian undercover agents are tracking the shipment, which is being moved by Arabic speaking men in an unspecified automobile on surface roads."

A sober silence filled the room as the allied military officers contemplated the challenges that were becoming more threatening by the hour. Above all, Jack thought, it was the uncertainty that jangled one's nerves. He would see Falk about it—with a new operational name, Justinian's Shield, after the 6th Century pandemic plague that had changed world history.

Jack's section now occupied the second floor of the building, except for Falk's suite of offices. Maro took over administration, while Lew Minchao was nominal commander. Jack was freed up to be the thinker and confessor of the outfit.

21.   Jogging—Cemetery Of Chagos Ghosts

Jack had for many years been an assiduous jogger in addition to be a martial arts expert and generally an athlete. He trained between and hour and two hours every day, running through kicks, punches, and other exercises.

He had always kept a kind of utility belt with a fanny pack or two on it, plus a small water bottle of metal in a Velcro holster—and a field knife, plus a compact Walther PPK/E snugly housed in an olive drab nylon holster. The weapons he kept in his rear fanny pack, the water on one hip, and the rest in his front pack.

After the loss of Team A, he had forced himself to make an hour or two a day for this, including a swim in the lagoon or the ocean. A few times, he took others along, but they rarely lasted at his pace. Maro, with her long legs, had come a few times, and she managed to keep up for a while, but usually fell out after the first five to seven miles. Jack was compact, wiry, and powerful. He had endurance and determination. Once he got into what he called autopilot, especially on the smooth roads around much of the island, he simply chugged along at a powerful clip. Don came twice, and dropped out. Lew Minchao came once, but didn't stand a chance.

This was a run he would have made with Ben Latoni, Ray Marston, or most visiting SEAL types. For the moment, he was on his own.

The day after the Europeans arrived, Jack was running along the eastern side of the atoll, heading north on the main road. As he came into the jungle area, where burros grazed in the clearings, he noticed something odd.

In the ghostly cemetery, he spotted what looked like a man.

He caught only a flash of facial skin. It was a small man.

Instantly alert, he slowed to a hesitant walk. He extracted the automatic from his fanny pack and held it at the ready against his right shoulder, with both hands, as he pressed himself in to the shadow of a large deciduous tree to reduce his own visibility. He was dressed in dark shorts, and a light top. Quickly, he stripped off the white top, down to the dark blue T-shirt underneath.

There.

A dark, slender figure flitted among the trees by the graves.

Jack thought he saw a bluish flash of light in the gloom.

Jack felt a creepy, crawly sensation, alone here in the cemetery with some type of person or creature that moved as if supernatural—silent, flitting, shadowy.

There it was again.

A figure moved against the tangled trees.

Again, he saw a flash of light, this time white.

As he moved forward, gun in hands, he saw the figure—a woman, small and agile, wearing black tights or form-fitting black sweat suit—breaking for open ground. Her form—shapely, athletic—was clearly visible for just an instant before she rose, scrabbling up a grassy knoll, and disappeared upward.

Jack ran as quietly as he could. He kept his eyes open in all directions, wary of ambush. What were the flashes of light he had spotted? A quick raking glance into the darkness behind him revealed nothing. Must have been some kind of electronic device—but what? And why?

He held his gun in his left hand while fumbling with his right in the front fanny pack. He always carried a cell phone for emergency. At the same time, he climbed up the warm grass and earth, to the top of a rise about ten meters or thirtyish feet above sea level.

For an instant, while he speed dialed his office, he looked about. He was atop a rise overlooking the old jungle plantation. Forest canopy stretched all around him for several square miles, though it would only be a half mile run to the seashore on the outside perimeter of the atoll.

Maro's voice sounded on the cell phone. "Hello? Jack?"

"Hold on." He stashed the phone in his fanny back before him.

At that moment, he saw the young woman again. She was a powerful sprinter, laying down yardage as she pumped away. She was on the beach, heading north toward the industrial zone and port there. He thought he recognized her. From his vantage point, he guessed that she was a light-skinned islander. With the kinky hair, he guessed she was not Filipina or other southeast Asian.

On impulse, he ran after her. He was a powerful runner, but he had trouble keeping up. She held her elbows and chin high, and ran in long, loping strides like a champion sprinter. That gave Jack an idea. If she was a sprinter, she would tire soon and have to slow down into a steady run. Jack entered his own autopilot zone, running for dear life. As the minutes went by, he gained his wind and fell into a smooth, steady stride. It was his normal fast run, a pace he could maintain for up to two miles before falling apart.

The beach looked picturesque ahead. The sand sloped downward to the right, where waves broke gently on the shore. Further out, breakers hit the edge of the local shelf underwater. The sea made a steady pulsing sound that alternated between heartbeats and thunder. The sand under Jack's feet shook each time a breaker fell apart in the nearby ocean. To his left ran a solid wall of jungle growth dark as night. Shells and other debris littered the beach along with blackened, drying kelp washed up during recent high tides. The young woman kept up a steady run about a thousand feet ahead. Where could she go to? If she ducked into the forest cover, he could call on Maro to get the base police out with choppers and bicycles. They would find her. She had no place to hide—as far as Jack knew. Why did she look familiar?

While running, he formulated a plan. It was desperate, but just crazy enough that it might work.

He had a lucky break when she stumbled and flew headfirst into the dirt. For a few seconds, she crawled about stunned. That let Jack catch up by a hundred feet or more. She picked herself up, a bit dazed, and began running again. A runner with her force, falling face first into sand—or gravel—could be seriously stunned and probably feeling as if she had been sandpapered into a bloody pulp. Had she hit her forehead on something? A rock?

Jack kept up a steady pace, pounding away on the sand so that his loose jaws jolted with each foot stride, and his cheeks fluttered as if someone were slapping him. He had a mile left in him. He knew that. She, on the other hand, was going slower. She was faltering. *Good.* She veered to her right and continued running along the hard sand at the water's edge, just above the mud line where water mixes with sand and softens it. The tide was going out, leaving higher ground damp and packed. She took advantage of that brown sugar to try and outrun him. But it wasn't working.

She stumbled once, dropping her hands nearly to the sand as her body made an agile recovery. She was young, he estimated no more than twenty or twenty-two. She had light coffee skin. When she glanced back, he saw an islander face, almost European, a mix probably, with slightly wide African nostrils and dark, desperate eyes the color of a meadow honey.

Now he recognized her: Nessie Galayan, the attractive, friendly young FNE woman from the BX cash register.

Within two minutes he tackled her. They went down together in the water. "Nessie, it's me."

"Leave me alone!" She started to kick and struggle, but he landed a fast, round-house punch from the hip, striking her on the right side, back of the head. That stunned her, and she lay gasping for wind, still with her knees up and her hands flat in a ready sprinting position—but she'd lost her spirit for the moment.

"Don't hurt me," she sputtered as she raised her head. Water poured off her face.

"Hold still. It's over." He sat on top of her, pinching her narrow waist with his knees. He pulled on her wrist to pin it behind her back. "I won't hurt you. Just lie still. Who are you really?"

"My name is Giselle Allan."

With a flash of insight, he guessed: "You are Chagossian."

She looked at him sullenly, sidelong. "Damn you."

He made a wild guess. "You came back to see the graves."

"None of your business."

"It is my business now. How did you get on the island?"

"I work here. You know that. Look in my bill fold. You will look anyway." She lay sprawled with her hands and legs flat down. In a way, she seemed to be resting after her desperate run.

He moved about, keeping the pressure on her, as he felt quickly for weapons.

She was clean—no gun, just a nasty looking little gutting knife, which he took from her and threw about twenty feet away into six inches of water for future reference if needed. Better to know where it was, in case she got frisky again.

She had a small, tight pocket—just a slit in her pants—and a thin leather wallet.

He fished it out and opened it.

There was her picture, only it said Nessie Galayan. "Fake Filipina name?"

"My married name."

"You said your name is Giselle."

"It's Giselle Vanessa Allan-Galayan. My husband is Filipino and we live in Manila."

Her identity card was from the Navy authority on Diego Garcia. Jack wondered if it was a forgery, or if she was simply a fake. He was tempted to call for police support, but had another idea.

"Nessie. You married a man to get on the island?"

"I love my husband, Edgardo. My people aren't allowed here, but his are. Is that stupid or what?"

"I agree it sounds pretty stupid," Jack said. "I saw the cemetery and I feel really bad for your people. What do I do with you now?"

"Let me go, Jack. My family want to see. My grandmother was born here, and she is dying. It will be one of the last things she sees. The last joy in her life, to see her parents' grave."

"All right," Jack said. As they spoke, he pulled her cell phone from her other pocket. "Are the photos on here?"

"Yes. Please. I will do anything for you. Don't erase them."

"I won't. I promise. You only need to tell the truth."

She relaxed, with a big collapsing sigh. "Thank you."

"Are you off work, Nessie?"

"On my lunch break."

"You sneaked out to take pictures."

"I've done it a few times. It is good for the soul."

"I understand. I agree. A lot of people are very sympathetic to your people. I feel sorry for what happened to them."

"I wasn't doing anything wrong," she said. "Not really."

"No you weren't," he said, without being sure.

"Yes," she said, starting to cry.

He did not trust her tears. They might be genuine, but she was a young woman on a mission, full of high energy, and she'd already deceived a lot of people. He manipulated her cell phone for a few seconds. "All right," he said. He threw her wallet and cell phone before her. "I'm going to get off you, and you are going to behave."

"I promise," she said. "You seem like a nice man."

"Here we go." Carefully, with one hand on the small of her back, he jumped away. He danced backward on the sand. "Okay, Nessie. Stand up." She scooped up her wallet and phone in one smooth motion and popped up into a standing position.

Jack stood twenty feet away, leaving her room to maneuver while he stayed out of her reach. "Go on," he said, feigning stupidity. "I know where you work. Send your pictures, go back to work, and stay out of trouble."

"Thank you," she said. "Can I go?"

"Take off," he told her.

She hardly looked at him, except for one strangely curious, disbelieving glance out of the corners of her eyes. Wiping tears away, she jogged away north on the beach.

Jack waited until she was far away.

Then, he took out his own cell phone.

He checked—and sure enough, he had called his own office number, which showed up under the innocuous listing Admin.

He had turned his cell phone to vibrate so she wouldn't suspect while they talked.

That meant he had her phone number dialed into his cell phone.

From here on, she could be tracked.

Jack called Maro and explained briefly what had happened.

"Oh, her," Maro said. "Smiley—I've seen her at the BX."

"It may be nothing, or it may be a lead or even a break. Get someone down on that number. Monitor every call she makes, any websites. Track her by GPS every move she makes. I want a report on anything you find out. Can you pick me up here?"

Though Maro outranked him, he was the functional commander of a new, as yet undefined, self-appointed mission—and she was good enough to understand. Maro was a team player who understood when it was time to lead, and when it was time to follow. This was Jack's show.

Meanwhile, an unsuspecting Giselle Nessie Allan-Galayan jogged out of sight. He felt certain in his gut that she was no terrorist. Maybe she was just photographing graves. Or someone had set her up to do something a little more. Or a lot more.

22.   Coming Into Focus—Horror a Life of Its Own

Minutes after Nessie had jogged away, a small helicopter came across the island, flying low. The chopper circled out to sea and set down on the beach near Jack.

Out stepped Maro, accompanied by a young blond, crew-cut man in blue jump suit with aviator sunglasses. The chopper pilot, similarly clad, waited inside his cockpit bubble.

Maro introduced the blond man: "Warrant Officer Two Stan Hancock, base security. He will be your shadow from here on in. Meet Captain Jack Dorsey, U.S. Army Reserve, Special Forces."

Jack shook hands with Hancock. "Nice to meet you, Chief."

"Pleasure, Sir."

"I'll be Jack, you be Stan."

"Good to go."

Maro said: "I'm going to get this chopper out of here. Admiral Falk will want a report."

"You go," Jack said. "Thanks for showing up so promptly. Tell Admiral Falk I'll give him a report as soon as I have a clue what is going on here."

As Maro took off in the chopper, Jack turned to Stan: "So I was out jogging, minding my own business, and I see this chick in the cemetery. She's dressed in black, acting suspicious, and I see some electronic flashes."

"Tourist?"

"Hardly. She claims she was taking photographs of the graves. I had her figured for Ilois by the skin color and the hair. Definitely not your vanilla Manila Filipino."

Stan looked a bit dubious. He seemed to be a skeptical, thoughtful man not given to accepting what he was told without a struggle. Jack liked that in a man. "There are thousands of islands in the Philippines and across the region. There are some kinky-haired folks in there."

"Right, well noted. However, she admitted it. She was here to photograph the graves for her grandmother, who is dying back in Seychelles."

"She said."

"I know, Stan. Bear with me. She was not entirely on the level. I got that much."

"Sorry."

"No, by all means, keep being a wise ass. I like talking to a thinking man instead of a robot. So here's the thing. Was she really photographing graves or were those flashes from some kind of electronic gadget that we would like to know about?"

"We'll have to comb the area."

"Right. Stan, I need a complete sweep of the area, especially the square mile centering on the cemetery—just in case she had some other business in there."

"You got it." Stan flipped open a cell phone, pressed a pre-dial, and started speaking. That done, he returned his attention to Jack. "We have some electronic warfare specialists on the way. They will take the place apart, literally and figuratively."

"Look for any kind of signal going in or getting out."

"Gotcha." Stan's cell beeped, and he answered. He told someone "Okay, thanks," and told Jack: "The chick is back on the job in the warehouse by the commissary. We are tracking her cell phone as you suggested."

"I would keep some eyeballs on her," Jack suggested.

"Okay, good idea." Stan spoke on the cell phone again. "Let me know," he concluded after a brief conversation. He told Jack: "That's one of my squad leaders, named Albert Duchy. Al is going to go plain clothes and visit the warehouse to check out your little islander."

"She's real cute," Jack said, "but a real drama queen. Tell your man not to let her go to his head."

"Right. You know, we probably have a major breach here when all is said and done."

"You better believe it," Jack said. "If she could get on the island and take pictures with a cell phone, what else do you have going on?" Privately he wondered—if people had thought differently half a century ago, would it have made more sense to enlist the Chagossian natives as allies and let them police their own island together with the U.S. Navy, rather than bringing in total, unknown alien foreigners from thousands of miles away, some of them from countries with Communist and Islamic insurgencies? Whatever...

Three gray vans pulled up with flashing orange lights. "The electronics sweepers," Stan said.

Jack felt his temper rising. "All right, Chief, listen to me. Can we be more subtle here? Have them hide those vehicles or send them back to base if possible. I don't know if someone is watching us, and if we are tipping them off that we are onto their game before we even know what they are up to, whoever they are."

Stan looked chastened. "I'm sorry, Jack. I'm trained as a cop, not James Bond. You're right. We'll go undercover."

Jack felt as though he'd suddenly discovered the key to Stan's thought processes. "That's right. We're going to be detectives."

"Duly noted," Stan said as he hurried off to speak with the technicians in fatigues, who waited with walkie-talkies and M-16s.

The cell chirped. It was Falk. "Jack, what is going on?"

"Sir, I was out jogging and—Maro can tell you the rest."

"She already did. It's a police matter. You get back here."

"Right. Only I have the woman's phone and GPS, and we need to track her. Please, I'm asking."

"Whatever you need, Jack, whatever you want. It's yours. Just come back here and hold my hand."

"I'm all yours, Admiral."

"All right, then I can come out from under the bed."

"You have Maro to hold your hand."

"I don't know what we would do without her; and Lew Minchao." Jack shook hands with Stan, gave him the number at the block house, and exchanged promises to keep in touch. The chopper returned to the east side of the atoll, picked Jack up, and carried him across to the airfield.

Upstairs, Falk stood with his fists wedged into his belt, and his compact, muscular body bouncing up and down on elastic-seeming feet. "I hear you had a run-in," he announced as Jack came up the concrete stairwell of the building. "Come in and brief me."

"I'll be over in a minute," Jack promised. In his offices, Jack found a dozen men and women, mostly the NATO officers who had arrived, with U.S. Navy enlisted clerks acting as typists and secretaries. Technicians were bringing in equipment to set up extra satellite relays for communication nets. It was a busy place.

Dr. Levine told him: "Captain, we are still tracking that truck filled with biological materials crossing Congo."

"How fast are they moving?" Jack asked.

Levine, who had changed out of his uncomfortable looking suit, now wore a totally tourist combination of Hawai'ian shirt, shorts with too many baggy pockets, and sandals; no socks. "We think they are making about thirty miles a day on surface roads."

"I wonder if it's a distraction," Jack said. "We are dealing with some slick characters here, our opponents. How did you find out about this shipment? And what is in it?"

"Actually," Levine said, "I walked into this situation and it hit me in the face. All I know is that I was handed a note and told we should track this vehicle. Apparently it consists of twelve corpses from a morgue back in Kinshasa, of people who died in the bush, from some sort of hemorrhagic fever, and were brought to the lab rather than burned in the fields."

"Keep tracking it," Jack said, "and anything else you may see."

An Italian colonel, Egidio Morelli of Rome, had been appointed spokesman for the Rapid Deployment Force officers. He told Jack: "We are monitoring European air space from A to Z. If a bee moves from one flower to another, our radars are tracking it. So far, nobody is coming anywhere near the Vatican or St. Paul's, and the football stadium in Paris is at half time, Morocco ahead by one goal but Dublin looking strong and may overtake them. A tense game."

"At this point in the playoffs, that's what you'd expect." Jack made it to his desk and managed to crank up his computer. His first action was always to check email—nothing from Temecula, meaning all was well with Catherine and the rest of the family. He flicked through the 300 or so messages, sending most to a Hold file.

You deleted nothing, in case something important was hidden amid the phishing and other junk that got through even secure military email servers. Minchao sent a personal note, proposing a walk on the beach early in the morning for fitness purposes. "Will do if available," Jack texted back.

As he became engrossed in his computer, his desk phone warbled softly. He picked up. "Dorsey."

"Captain, it's Stan."

"Yeah."

"She is missing."

"Who?" It took him a second to change focus. "Of course, the girl on the beach. Galayan."

"We can't find her. We found her phone—in her locker, with the padlock loose. It looks like she flew the coop—or something happened to her."

"Turn the island upside down. We want her."

"I'm on it."

"What about her husband, Mr. Galayan?"

"We have checked him out and he's missing too."

"What do we know?"

"Edgardo Galayan of bla bla address, Mindanao. He's 35 years old, clean record, Roman Catholic, two years of college in Manila, four years' service as an electronic technician in the Philippine Navy, followed by, if you're interested, several stable looking jobs over the years. By the way, I have ONI here—there is a Commander Roger Lewis on the investigation now."

"Good," Jack said. "What more do we know about Galayan?"

"That he is married."

"We knew that."

"But not to our missing Giselle. His wife is one Marta Confesion, age 32, living in Mindanao and mother of his five children. Unless they are polygamists, Mr. Galayan is not married to Nessie. What's worse, he is missing as well, so we can't sort of talk with him to get to the bottom of things."

"Ouch," Jack said. "Well, at least we have an open Pandora's Box going on. Keeps life interesting. Anything out of that cemetery?"

"Not a peep. Technicians are covering every inch of ground, looking for anything suspicious. I don't have much hope. We cracked Nessie's cell phone—nothing but pictures of graves."

"Got names on those graves?"

"A few, maybe. I'm not sure."

"Analyze the names. See if we have a pattern—maybe a family of Ilois, back in Seychelles. Someone must know this woman. She had that kind of French sounding accent that I've heard on some of the islanders in YouTube videos and what not."

"I'm on it, Jack. I'll let you know the minute anything pops up."

"Good job, Stan. Stay on top of it."

After ringing off, he went into Falk's office, upended a meeting the admiral was having with some very important looking logistics officer types. "What's up, Jack?"

"I need to brief you on this woman. It's now an ongoing investigation."

Falk had Jack sit down, and heard his report. "Puzzling," was his conclusion. "What about Europe and Flight 777?"

"I have my doubts about a Europe scenario. We have that whole RDF crew all over it. I can't imagine that a plane could move anywhere in Europe without being nailed by fighter planes from a half dozen countries in five minutes."

"That's my impression," Falk said. "Good thing Naples stepped into this pile of manure with both boots. I'm getting that feeling: out of control, heads gotta roll feeling; suddenly, I'm just a runner in the game, not the owner or the coach."

"Maybe the entire plane thing was a diversion," Jack said.

"Or maybe Camp Zero was the whole point. Maybe the other team stopped playing, and we're just kicking the ball around here on overtime." Falk picked up a control wand and clicked it at his wall monitor. The flat screen flickered into life. CNN banners rolled across the screen as an anchor in London spoke: "Allied forces are engaged in a major annual exercise, testing the readiness of NATO's Rapid Deployment Force. As part of the games, the U.S. Sixth Fleet is moving two carrier battle groups into position— one in the Mediterranean, the other near Diego Garcia on its way to the Persian Gulf region."

Jack and Falk stared at the television for a minute.

Then they looked at each other.

Jack said: "We have a carrier group headed here?"

Falk nodded. "Arrives off the atoll tomorrow noon. Why?"

"I didn't know."

"Jack, you are making me nervous."

"I am making myself nervous, Sir. Can they hit the carrier somehow?"

"With what?"

"The missing airliner?"

"You're nuts."

"Pray that I am."

"I still think it's in Africa under a giant, sandy tarp."

Jack pulled out his phone, accessed the Internet, and did a quick calculation. "Khartoum to Colombo, Sri Lanka—that's about 3,300 miles, or 5,300 klicks."

"What are you saying, Jack?"

"About six or seven hours' flight time."

"Come on."

"Sir, we can't afford to take a chance. If the carrier battle group is due off Diego Garcia at noon tomorrow…"

Falk leaned across his desk, pressed an intercom, and said: "Chief, I want the exact ETA for that CVN ASAP."

The voice outside said: "Got it, Sir. Ten a.m. in the morning, give or take some minutes. We can track it exactly if you need."

"Get me the exact ETA and stand by. Keep tracking."

"Yessir."

Jack said: "It's eight p.m. here, meaning the carrier is already within about a hundred miles of here. If someone were to hit it, they could be doing it right now."

Falk blanched. "I'll be talking with a two or three star admiral on a command ship traveling with that battle group. I had better have something solid to offer for him to go on a lockdown status."

"I have a feeling something is going to happen."

"Me too," Falk admitted and pressed the intercom button. "Chief, I need to talk to the admiral on the command ship in person. First, set me up with Captain Antonov here on the island."

"Yessir. I'll set that up right away."

"I happen to be the ranking Navy officer on Diego Garcia at the moment," Falk said. "Still, I'd better go through channels. I'll see what the CO says." The Captain in charge of the island functionally outranked the Admiral in this instance. Captain Stuart Antonov answered. "Hey, Paul, what are you up to?"

"Stu, I'm up to my eyeballs in alligators and need your advice."

"Grab your rear end with both hands and run for your life," came the other man's voice. "Any other questions?"

"We are working this missing woman case alongside your base security. I am requesting that we be informed in parallel to your chain of command about every development in the case, since I think it affects our mission here."

"Not a problem. I'll signal my folks to copy you ASAP on any developments."

"Thank you. I think that covers it."

"Seriously."

"Seriously, Stuart. We have a very sticky situation, maybe."

"I see," came the dry voice. "The other half of that is maybe not."

"That's the really sticky part. I don't know."

"Don't know what."

"Don't know if the aircraft carrier heading our way is about to get hit."

"Ouch. And you have something solid to go on."

"No, I don't. Your base police are chasing a missing woman that our friend Jack Dorsey captured on the beach, acting very strange in the cemetery, and now she is missing. So is her husband who is not really her husband. We are investigating it under the umbrella of Operation Lima Triple, which is officially defunct but like the sticky thing, not really."

"Ah, Jeez. Just when I was about to relax for the night with my reruns of NCIS. Run the whole thing by me again, slowly."

Jack took a chair, backwards, waiting as Paul Falk told the story to Captain Antonov.

Antonov's measured response was: "All right, here is what we'll do. I'll call the command ship, talk to the admiral—he and I went to Annapolis together—and I'll just tell him we're chasing our tails here, but we are worried about his ship, and can he increase his defensive measures a notch. That way, he's tipped off. He'll understand. We'd be derelict not to at least give him a heads-up. And don't worry—he has a lot on his plate. They play games like this all day long. He'll think it's a good training exercise."

"Thanks, Stu. You always know what to do."

"Call me anytime. You owe me a handicap next time we play."

"Done deal, buddy."

They rang off. Falk relaxed a bit. "All right, at least we have tipped off the players, and Antonov will field the ball for us with Fleet. We are just staff jockeys here, after all. He is directly in the command hierarchy. So." He tapped his knuckles sharply on the desk. "I guess I will be pulling an all-nighter here with the NATO stiffs. They haven't had a good war on their hands since Adolf shot himself, so they can lose a little sleep. Meanwhile, Jack, I want you to stay on top of this missing woman thing along with base security. They'll be reporting up their chain of command. I want us to be in on everything that goes down. You be my deputy dog in that hunt."

"Right."

Jack walked down to see Maro, who was still at her desk. "We're in for an all nighter."

"Oh-oh," she said. "I was expecting that." She shuffled papers busily among her in and out boxes.

"Can we get a driver?"

"Jessica Napoleon's pulling duty. I'll have her bring the Jeep around and stand by for orders."

"Have the chopper standing by as well."

"Yessir."

"I'm sorry."

"That's okay. You be in charge for a while. I need a rest."

"If I step on your toes, just let me know."

"Trust me, I'm not shy." She was his superior, and would probably write his performance review to be signed off by Falk. He wasn't too worried, but he didn't want to bruise her ego—he liked her too much as a person. "Jack, do the job. This time you lead, I follow unless I think you're making a wrong turn. I'll let you know. Let's get it done."

Falk buzzed. Jack and Maro walked down the hall to see him. Outside, night had fallen. The Milky Way made a sweep of stars across the clear Indian Ocean sky.

In his office, Falk said: "I just talked to a guy I know back in CONUS. He is an expert on this stuff. How would anyone get near an aircraft carrier?"

"It would not be easy," Jack said.

Falk gesticulated. "Defensive measures—they fly choppers around as decoys. They shoot missiles. They fly dozens of jets hundreds of miles around as a shield. They can detect mines and other underwater armaments. Plus they have Phalanx."

Phalanx, sometimes called R2-D2 because it resembles the comical robot in Star Wars, is a radome-topped piece of equipment about the size of a car standing on end, shaped like a cylinder. It has a Gatling gun, borrowed from Vietnam era technology. The Phalanx CIWS (Close-In Weapons System) is an important shipboard defense against anti-ship missiles and other incoming attack weapons. It functions as a radar-guided 20 millimeter (0.79 inch) by 102 mm Gatling gun mounted on a swiveling base capable of rotating 300 degrees horizontally and between 85 and minus 25 degrees vertically. It unleashes a torrent of armor-piercing tungsten rounds at a rate of 4,500 rounds per minute or 75 rounds/second from pre-loaded belts feeding six barrels. It shoots at a muzzle velocity of 100 meters or 3,600 feet per second over an effective firing range of about 3.6 km or 2.2 miles.

Falk said: "The Phalanx defensive system alone, in plain English—there's nothing it can't shred within a mile of the ship in ten seconds of solid firing, including a Boeing 777 crazy enough to venture close. That's not counting missiles and other defenses. Sounds like a dinosaur roaring, with echoes off the horizon."

"I've been thinking about it," Jack said. "There is only one way, and that would be to drop the airliner straight down on them from 35,000 feet."

"You've got to be kidding me."

"I wish I were. This never really entered my mind until the last few days, and I'm just thinking it through now. You could hide a 777 in the swarm of ten thousand or more jets up in the air at any moment. If you could target precisely, you could have your suicide pilots fly to a coordinate directly above the aircraft carrier. Assume the plane is loaded with everything from jet fuel to gasoline or napalm to high explosives. It would fall about seven miles, and hit its target in less than a minute at an almost unimaginable mass and speed."

"What about the defensive weapons?"

"You'd have almost zero warning time. Your only hope would be whatever defensive aircraft you have in the air at the moment, and they'd have to be ready to fire in the correct direction."

"What about Phalanx?"

"For that you would front-load your airplane with a bunch of lumber—maybe a stack of railroad ties. Coming down at 90 degrees, you'd actually be out of range of the Phalanx' maximum upward angle of 85%. Assume for a moment they got some Phalanx rounds in—the lumber or other ballast would absorb it. Remember, it's just a falling dumb bomb at this point, not a flying aircraft. The pilots are still steering it to jihad heaven with all seventy virgins lifting their veils and swaying from side to side—but if you shredded the cockpit, the thing turns into a falling can of explosives. Once it hits the carrier deck, it drops all the way through and breaks the keel, sinking her in minutes. You'd take out about six thousand people, double what they killed on 9/11. Mission accomplished."

Falk stared at him. "That's crazy."

"I know. These people are stark raving mad. And they have nothing better to do all day but figure out how to destroy things and kill innocent people."

Falk said: "If they have other ships in the carrier battle group running alongside with their Phalanxes ready, they could shred the thing as it's coming down. They'd still get debris on deck, maybe take out the ship anyway."

"Or damage it enough to put it out of action," Jack said.

"Not a desirable state of affairs. Not a place to let things get to." He buzzed the Chief again. "Get me Captain Antonov ASAP."

Admiral Falk ran the scenario by Captain Antonov, who made groaning and whistling noises. Antonov promised: "I will call the command ship right away. They need to be on standby just in case."

As Jack calculated, the hit could come at any moment. Ideally, the timing would be as the carrier group approached within sight of Diego Garcia. That would add incalculable propaganda value, whatever the outcome of the mission itself.

To hit that spot in a timely fashion, the plane would launch— from, say, Khartoum, Sudan as a reference point—six or seven hours ahead of time. That meant a takeoff in Sudan, or in the Great Sand Sea of Libya and Egypt, by three a.m., but no telling if the flight was already in the air now, and drawing close.

"That brings us to one last critical point," Jack said.

"I'm all ears," Falk said, with the phone on one ear.

"This is going to happen at night if it happens, so how do they target it precisely? Obviously, they have to have some sort of electronic targeting system. A system like that emits pings or signals of some type. We need to have the technical people standing by in case the signals come from this island, or most likely a ship off the coast."

Falk stood up. "All right, Jack. I'll go for it."

Within the hour, electronic ears were eavesdropping on the entire wave spectrum surrounding Diego Garcia, both from shipboard and from land-based units.

Civil aviation agencies were polled across the entire British Indian Ocean Territories—there were hundreds of major flights criss-crossing Indian Ocean air space, centering near Diego Garcia. Sea and air lanes proliferated between Africa, India, Indonesia-Malaysia, Australia, and even Antarctica—including passenger airliners, military aircraft of various nations, and cargo craft including UPS and FEDEX carriers; and an endless swarm of surface vessels.

Jack saw that a swarm of helicopters hovered on the horizon, low around the carrier group. All sailors and Marines on board were on full alert at their battle stations. Aircraft from Diego Garcia and other islands in the region lifted off to survey the waters for any possible intruder ships, however small. Coastal vessels roared out to sea to check on fishing fleets in the area.

At midnight came messages from headquarters in both Naples and Stuttgart, stating that an Egyptian air force patrol had spotted the missing Flight 777's probable location in the Libyan desert, far from civilization in the remote southeast sand sea bordering the far west of Egypt, the bleak Shamalya region in the northwest of Sudan, and the wilderness of northern Chad. A reconnaissance pilot had flown out within the hour and set down on the hard, flat ground. This was the type of terrain where the famous U.S. bomber *Lady Be Good* was lost on a patrol in 1944, and not found until 1958. Its crew members, having survived the desert crash, had walked to their deaths from thirst in the harsh and unforgiving terrain—an area as large as any European nation. The patrol found evidence that dozens of men had lived there, but had now left by overland routes, probably by truck toward Somalia on the Red Sea. Their mission was completed, which had begun on a deserted road in Myanmar (Burma) two months earlier, had taken them to Equatorial Africa where they had staged the infamous run-up to the Camp Zero debacle, and then a successful stint sitting under cover in the Libyan desert. During this time, Libya in particular and the region in general was in political and military turmoil, lending added cover to the terrorists. Now only the two suicide pilots were needed for the seven hour flight eastward across the Indian Ocean on a plane repainted to resemble perhaps an Australian, an Indonesian, or perhaps a New Zealand aircraft.

In the search for any clue about Nessie Galayan, Maro had tracked down her family--using the names on the graves in her photos. With the help of U.S. Consular officials, a discreet local Seychellois police detective had tracked down Giselle's family in the capital, Port Victoria, on Mahé Island. She'd found an elderly man, who spoke with her from his home via satellite hookup. His name was Victor Allan, the grandfather of Giselle Vanessa Allan-Galayan. "We are beside ourselves," Victor Allan said in clear but accented English. A younger woman, an aunt of Giselle, helped translate because his native language was a French Creole patois. "Vanessa married this older man from the Philippines to get away from here, from our poor living conditions, and she was always proud and stubborn. She has sent us pictures of our ancestral graves. We love her and are very proud of her, but—Lady, Mister, can you bring her back to us unharmed? We would be ever so grateful to you."

"We promise we will do everything we can," both Maro and Jack promised in profusion. The old man's kindness and wisdom touched them very deeply, as did his proud bearing under a number of obvious strains, not the least of which was caring for a dying mother, and dealing with rebellious younger generations.

During the early morning hours, U.S. Navy Shore Patrol units found Giselle Allan locked in a cellar in a deserted blockhouse on the northeast tip of Diego Garcia. She was scared, but unharmed. A chopper flew her to Stan Hancock's base security headquarters on the northwest tip of the atoll. There, as Stan related by phone to Jack, the young Chagossian woman spilled the truth to Stan's investigators. Jack spoke with her briefly as well by phone, telling her of his conversation with Victor Allan. This brought Giselle or Nessie to genuine tears—a bath of them, from what Jack could hear over the phone. She promised to help Jack and the authorities as best she could, in return for a well-intentioned promise to put in a good word for her people.

She had undertaken a personal odyssey, without the approval of her family, out of youthful outrage and idealism. After being contacted by a certain Mr. Galayan, who was trawling Seychelles for a prospective, useful woman among the Chagossian population, Nessie had agreed to a fake marriage that would get her access to Diego Garcia as Edgardo Galayan's alleged wife. In return for spending several days photographing the grave sites, she had agreed to bury an electronic signaler atop the grassy hill near the cemetery.

Jack knew exactly where this was, and gave instructions to Stan's technical troops. Oddly enough, the gadget—which Giselle described as a dull metal sphere the size of a volley ball, with one short telescoping antenna—was not putting out any signals. Jack suggested that Stan have his people locate it, using metal detectors if necessary, but not to disturb it for the time being—merely to observe, and be ready to blow it up at a moment's notice, but to study it in case any clues about the larger plot could be derived.

Following up with Philippine authorities in Mindanao and Manila, U.S. intelligence put together a snap profile on Edgardo Galayan. He was business partners with his slightly older brother, a U.S.-educated electrical engineer and electronics expert, Delberto Galayan. This man was CEO of a company in Mindanao that did R&D on economical new low-end drone aircraft. He was also a fervent convert to a fanatical sect of Islam, and belonged to a separatist group seeking independence from Manila.

"What do you know?" Jack said to Maro. "I wonder if he is one of those FNE guys flying model airplanes up on the northeast end of the atoll."

"Right on the beach, within view of the ocean," Maro said. "They were planning toward this moment the whole time."

A quick internet search revealed a combination of hobby air craft and other activities, including a six foot long model airplane powered by sophisticated miniature alcohol burning engines. Better yet, the company produced a kind of subsurface torpedo drone that ran on battery power, with a life span of at least twenty hours, at a depth of one fathom or about six feet. It was made of a radar-deflecting ceramic material and sold to several regional navies. It could carry either explosive charges, or radar arrays, or signaling devices as needed, and ran in stealth mode. One of the models had turned up in the Thai special forces' search in Burma for the 777's landing strip on Ramree Island.

"That's our candidate," Falk told Jack as they collated the information. "No idea how you attack a carrier with a model airplane, but we're all ready for the nut house, so lay it on me."

Lew Minchao agreed, looking on over their shoulders. "Too much coincidence." Lew was coordinating the conversation between Captain Antonov, Falk's office, the captains at sea including the fleet admiral, and various agencies on land. By now, NSA and other big players were totally focused in, and in Washington—Jack and Falk bet—POTUS was being dragged out of bed or whatever to the Situation Room in the White House. All the lights were burning at Kelley Barracks in Stuttgart, the USNSA in Naples, and other headquarters and hot spots around the world.

"Flight 777 is in the air and drawing close," Maro announced as she performed her own calculations with pen, steno pad, and cell phone. "There are 35 large aircraft flying within a hundred miles of us. It's near dawn, and traffic patterns are very busy."

"Pull as many of them off course as possible," Falk ordered. "The clearer the sky, the more readily we'll be able to spot 777 as it comes closer."

Maro directed a group of NCOs to start calling regional TCAs.

Antonov came by, in fatigue uniform, with a troop of staff and aides. "The carrier group is in full evasive maneuvers. Everything is up and flying. They're as ready as they'll ever be," said Antonov.

"Can the bastard get through?" Jack tersely wondered out loud.

"That is the question of the hour," Admiral Falk seconded.

"Everything hangs on it," Antonov agreed.

"Oh my God," Maro said.

"What?"

"We have a bogey at five miles and closing, altitude 35,000 feet," intoned a technician at a corner console.

Maro said: "The cemetery. There is now a signal coming out. I just had a call from Stan Hancock's people on the grassy hill."

"Tell them not to touch it," a tech said. "It's triangulating. They have at least two, maybe three or four, other stations in the area. If we can pick them up, we can locate the critical one at sea on the other side of the carrier group. Galayan is somewhere—either on the island or on a boat out there—manipulating a drone."

"You think he's flying a drone?" Falk asked.

"It's our best bet," the chief said. "We're low on options."

"Does he have to be on top of the carrier group?" Falk asked.

An electronics NCO spoke up. "Not too close, Sir. As long as they have at least one data point each on axes x and y, plus a third axis z to delta their altitude, they can tell the plane to drop anywhere inside their Cartesian coordinate plane."

A tekkie woman added: "The points should be at least ten miles apart, and preferably on opposite sides of the target; meaning something out at sea, exchanging signals with the primary."

"So where is the primary operator?" Jack asked.

"We have the one node above the cemetery," Falk said. "Let's find at least one more."

The electronics chief said: "One of them has to be out at sea beyond the ship—a transceiver on a small boat maybe? But wait, I am getting a signal here on Diego Garcia. Not the cemetery, but up near the Point."

"You mean northwest?"

The chief nodded. "At the lagoon entrance."

Stan was in the room, meeting with Minchao. Stan said: "I have armed patrols combing every inch of ground. If Galayan is hiding someplace, we'll find him."

Minchao said gently: "We should have found him already. Let's focus to the north of here, on those three small islands."

The chief pointed out: "We may be able to ping him with the cemetery equipment. These things have to talk to each other."

"Get on it," Falk said.

"Hurry, hurry," Maro said. "There are three aircraft closing in at 35,000 feet. One of them has to be the killer plane Triple Seven."

"I am getting a fix on our north," the chief said. "Not exactly clear yet, but we are zeroing in."

Jack said: "I'm going to hit the ground and start running. Maro, where is that chopper?"

She looked up. "Outside on the pad, feathering. Where are you going?"

"I am going to head for the islands in the mouth of the bay. It's as good a shot as any. Keep me posted."

He sprinted down the stairs, two at a time, holding a shotgun.

Maro followed right behind him, carrying Dischler's Glock and a green canvas bag full of ammo handed to her by Falk's MCPO.

The chopper was sitting on a concrete square outside with its engine churning softly. As they ran toward it, Jack waved his arm in a circular motion, and the pilot started throttling up. The engine burst into a loud whine, and bluish smoke mushroomed out as the blades started whipping around ever faster.

No sooner had Jack and Maro boarded than the lone pilot gave them the high sign and started upward. Jack and Maro just had time to buckle in as the chopper tilted forward and rose into the air.

Jack shouted instructions at the pilot to head for the islands in the mouth of the bay. The man nodded and took the craft up fast and steep. The flight took five minutes at a racing, tilted attitude.

En route, they got information from Falk's staff. "There is a signal coming from an abandoned well on the middle island. The well is capped with a heavy steel door. We'll meet you there. Chief Hancock's people will get it open for you."

Dawn blossomed as Jack and his companions clattered through the sky. A reddish-yellow tropical sun burst up from the eastern sky over the water, creating myriad golden-red ripples. The deceptively peaceful scene made its reality ever more grotesque.

The carrier battle group steamed out at sea, just on the horizon visible from the chopper's perspective, flying at 800 feet. Soon, the chopper hovered over the middle island in the harbor mouth, looking for a spot to set down.

Jack noted intense white streamers of foam as the ships out on the horizon went through intense evasion maneuvers.

Another chopper flew in low and set down nearby.

Jack's pilot set down in ankle-deep water in the shallow lagoon entrance. A half dozen sailors armed with machine guns and shotguns piled out of the chopper. Two of them carried an ammo box between them—containing explosives.

Ahead in the grass and sand was a concrete pillbox sealed all around. Jack saw no exterior sign of what might be lurking inside. The sailors banged on the steel door, with no result.

Jack and Maro's chopper lifted off toward the main atoll, out of harm's way.

The sailors set their charge, yelled "Fire in the hole!", and ducked backward around the concrete corner of the structure. Jack and Maro flattened themselves in the damp, cold grass face down.

The charge blew with a deafening explosion, half ripping the door to expose a dimly lit interior beyond its mangled steel. Smoke drifted in the air as the ground chief exchanged signals with Jack.

Jack hefted his six-gauge pump action shotgun and plunged forward. He must go in first to judge what Galayan had going on in there. The fate of thousands of sailors and Marines might depend on what he decided to do when he saw Galayan.

Maro followed closely behind him, also wielding a shotgun and the satchel of reloads. Behind them came the armed sailors.

They clattered down a flight of concrete steps, into a large underground room lit by lamps in steel grills on the walls. Evidently this was an old storage shed designed to stay waterproof, and holding electrical circuits and sea rescue equipment, as Jack gauged with a quick look around.

At a table in the center sat a single man, manipulating electronic equipment. From pictures, Jack recognized Edgardo Galayan, who sat before several computer monitors, system units, and sending equipment. An animation ran, showing showed a simulation of his company's underwater stealth torpedo—not an exploder, but a ceramic-sheathed transponder in motion. Galayan was clearly guiding it around the aircraft carrier. The moving underwater device was exchanging triangulation signals with the cemetery station and this island. On the animation, Jack also saw a vertical, z-axis delta indicator hovering in mid-air. The vertical still held steady, so the plane had not begun to drop. But the x and y coordinates were closing in on each other. The z-coordinate turned red and began to flash on and off.

"Galayan, shut it down!" Jack shouted.

"Go to hell!" Galayan said—focused and never looking up.

"He also has a drone airplane on the horizon for redundancy," Maro said. "Look." She pointed to a computer screen off to one side, where another animation showed a large model airplane hovering like a mosquito on the vast ocean horizon.

"Galayan!" Jack shouted.

At that moment, they heard voices relayed by radio from Admiral Falk's offices. Somehow, Galayan had managed to tune in to the island's communication network so he could gloat over his accomplishments as people would begin to cry out in dismay.

"Bogey at 35,000 feet. We have him on radar. Jets are scrambled and ready to fire missiles but they can't make it on time. He just started his down turn. He is diving. He is coming down. In less than a minute he'll hit his target."

Jack's eyes followed the cabling out of the concrete cellar.

Time for a quick decision. Should he sever the line snaking up the concrete wall, thus cutting off all signals coming from the bunker?

That z-coordinate was the only hope. What if he could still take it off course?

Using the shotgun, he blew Galayan into smithereens. Blood and gore covered the concrete wall, mixing with moss and fungus there in the sickly light.

Jack threw himself forward and manipulated the joy sticks.

Galayan had three of them going. If he hit the right one—he jiggled them all.

"Look!" came a shout.

It was too late to run up the stairs and look.

On a monitor, which Galayan had set up for his own delight and enjoyment, the missing Boeing 777 could be seen falling from the sky.

It would become an image of global importance, as iconic and forever as the footage of the jets on 9/11 flying into the Twin Towers in New York City on live news television.

For half a long minute, the huge machine tumbled toward the sea.

Slowly, it turned.

One by one, jet fighter missiles shot its large wings off.

The roar of a half dozen Phalanx Gatling gun systems on support ships echoed with eerie force across the sea.

The aircraft was by now simply a falling dumpster of metal and lumber, loaded with flammable liquids and high explosives.

Could it still be steered? The terrorists' calculation was that it must not be capable of diversion as it fell. They knew U.S. Navy defensive systems might be operational in those split seconds.

Jack still lay sprawled over the desk, holding a joy stick in each hand.

The targeting monitors in front of him flashed red and white alarm signals.

What to do?

Had must throw the plane off course, or the aircraft carrier would become a raging inferno in the next half minute.

Jack could see it falling, a brightly flaming dot trailing a corkscrew spiral of black smoke.

Its cockpit was totally gone—shot away—leaving only a stub fuselage with piles of oily lumber and debris falling with the plane or slightly ahead of it.

A huge shout rose from countless throats.

Jack had one hope. Somewhere in that falling mass, protected until the last moment, must be the z-delta sensor.

And Jack held the joystick for that transponder signal in his hand, with a long black twisted pair wire running across the table, braided into the other joystick control wires, and running up the bare concrete wall.

Taking Maro's twelve gauge, Jack fired a deafening round at the wall. His shot sprayed blinding concrete chips all over the room while it severed the joystick wires.

On board the plummeting cadaver plane, deeply embedded amid its explosive cargo, a tiny receiver perceived a change in signal—the absence of signal—and interpreted this to mean that it had reached the deck of the carrier.

At 3,000 feet, the aircraft exploded.

Pieces of lumber and metal flew in all directions. A huge fire ball shone like a hazy, brilliant sun over the carrier. Some of its parked aircraft crumbled and blew away into the sea. All the windows in the bridge blew out, and bodies on deck twirled like broken match sticks.

But the main brunt of the deadly bomb had been spent.

And the blazing, crippled tangled of wreckage began to twirl out of control, missing the aircraft carrier in its last seconds of descent.

Spiraling dizzyingly, the cadaver of Flight 777 crashed into open ocean less than 1,000 feet from the carrier. It exploded again on impact, sending debris flying in all directions—but the remaining charges were weak, and water cushioned the effect. Most of what flew up was vapor and spray from thousands of pounds of high explosive.

The aircraft carrier swayed sideways on the monitors in the bunker. For two or three minutes of chagrin, Jack thought it would heel over and be swamped. It would fill with water and sink. But it did not. Slowly, over the next ten minutes, as the waters stopped roiling, as the last bits of Flight 777 sank beneath the waves, the carrier battle group emerged virtually unscathed. There were some injuries, and ultimately two dozen dead sailors and Marines. A few aircraft were destroyed in place or lost over the side. It had been a close call. But the odyssey of the vanished Flight 777 had at last come to a merciful end.

24. Epilog

With the completion of his mission, Jack was free to return home. Within a day or two, he would hang up his Army uniform and revert to Reserve status, on inactive status for the next critical mission if one were to arise.

Catherine was due any moment and she confided in a phone call, just before Jack took off from Diego Garcia on a standby C-17 flight headed for Honolulu and then San Diego, that they were about to have a baby girl.

The carrier battle group steamed past Diego Garcia, essentially intact except for serious repairs that could be made underway from a supply ship. The European Union-NATO Rapid Deployment Force exercise went off without a hitch, including U.S. carrier battle groups in the Med and near the Persian Gulf.

POTUS, State, and the Chairman of the Joint Chiefs went live at the White House for a press briefing with an air of subdued triumph—it had been a very close call, and the world knew it. Nobody was dancing on the streets of any Third World capital. The perpetrators who had put the missing airliner plot into motion were still at large, and needed to be found. A worldwide manhunt would usher in the next phase of the war to save civilization from its enemies foreign and domestic, crazy and crazier. The investigation was already underway, starting with those who had sold the stolen passports in Paris.

Maro hugged Jack tightly on the tarmac at Diego Garcia, and he held her long, shapely form tightly before letting go. He shook hands with Lew Minchao, who relayed the information that Ben Latoni was sitting up in bed at Landstuhl and asking for a coconut milkshake—and for status on his friends. Jack sent word that he would visit with Ben in the United States, and they'd make a trip together to visit Ray Marston's widow and children in St. Louis, Missouri.

Paul Falk escorted Jack as far as the tail gate of the C-17. "If you ever want to go active duty again, I will always have a billet for you," Falk promised.

"But I'm in the Army, Sir."

"Never mind mere details," Falk said. "We get the job done."

They shook hands.

"I have a call in to the President of Seychelles," Falk said. "And also Washington, D. C. I have some friends in high places. I'll see if we can get the ball rolling to replace some of these FNEs with Chagos Islanders. It's about time, I would say."

Jack thought of Victor Allan. "I don't think we could find a more loyal and helpful group of people to help us run the island."

"Yes," Maro said, "and we're sending Nessie home as promised. She spilled the beans on Galayan, and we consider it a wash with her misguided work for her phony husband."

As a red sunset filled the Indian Ocean, and the stars came out above its rippling waters, Jack's powerful C-17 smoothly lifted into the stratosphere and headed east, racing with the line between nightfall and daylight.

Sitting strapped in, backwards, he pulled out his cell phone and made a call.

"Yes?" said a tired but happy voice.

"Baby, it's me."

"Jack, are you coming home?"

"Yes."

"Cuddle with me," she said.

"Okay. Pick a song, and we'll whisper it together as we go to sleep together."

Map Section

The following are selected maps (Source: CIA) to help readers visualize the geographical sweep of the story. Further maps and information are available online at many free resources including the CIA World Fact Book (www.cia.gov/), Wikipedia (wikipedia.org/), and more.

In place of distance legend on many maps, I offer the following approximate (rounded) flight distances obtained from Wikipedia, MapQuest, GoogleMaps, WorldAtlas, and other online resources.

The numbers representing approximate straight-line air distances are presented thus: [U.S. miles (mi); universal kilometers (km); generously rounded upward hours' flight time at a presumed 500 mph (800 kph) flight speed for a Boeing 777 at 35,000 ft cruising altitude]. Again: distances and times are listed approximate for clarity. Read: [mi, km, hrs].

Kuala Lumpur and Ho Chi Minh City [600, 960, 2]

Kuala Lumpur and Beijing, China [2650, 4300, 6]

Kuala Lumpur and Penang, Malaysia [160, 260, 1]

Kuala Lumpur and Ramree Island, Burma (Myanmar) [1200, 2000, 3]

Ramree Island region and Maldives Islands [1900, 3000, 4]

Ramree Island region and Diego Garcia [2300, 3800, 5]

Maldives and Diego Garcia [560, 900, 1]

Diego Garcia and Seychelles Islands [1200, 1900, 3]

Diego Garcia and Nairobi, Kenya [2500, 4000, 5]

Nairobi, Kenya and Central African Republic (C.A.R.) [3700, 5900, 8]

C.A.R. and Khartoum, Sudan [1000, 1600, 2]

Khartoum and Jerusalem [1100, 1800, more precisely 2.2 hours]

Khartoum and Straits of Hormuz [1750, 2800, more precisely 2.5 hours]

Khartoum and Rome, Italy [2200, 3500, 5]

Khartoum and Paris, France [2850, 4600, 6]

Khartoum and London, U.K. [3100, 5000, 6]

Khartoum, Sudan & Diego Garcia [3100, 5000, more precisely 5.2 hours]

Dark arrow points to Diego Garcia.

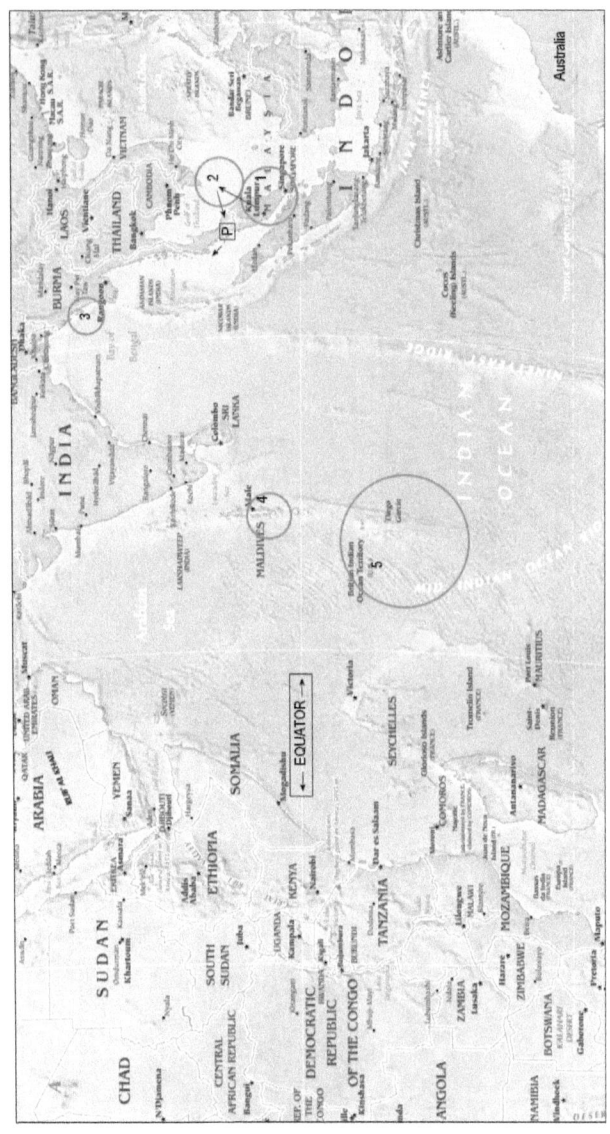

1. KUL, 2. Turn over G of Thailand, P. Penang radar; 3. Ramree Burma,
4. Maldives sighting, 5. Diego Garcia, Note: Equator line shown.

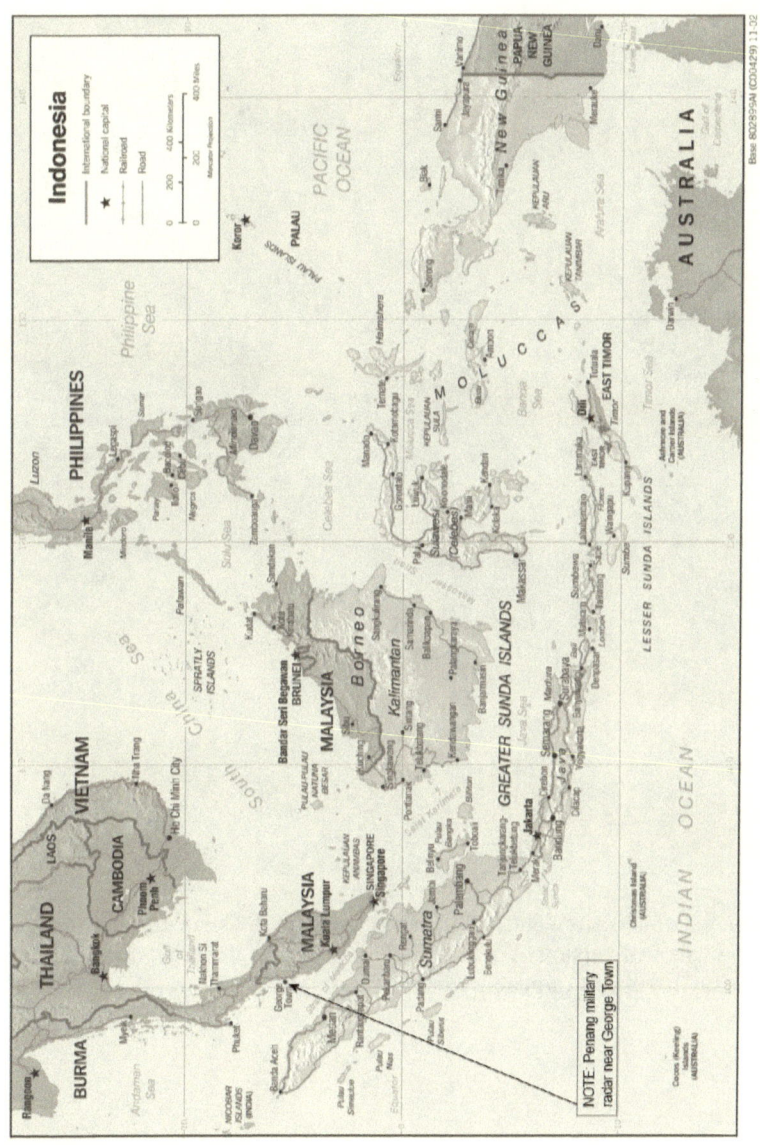

Southeast Asia, depart Kuala Lumpur Intl Airport (KUL); arrow points to the military radar site at Penang near George Town.

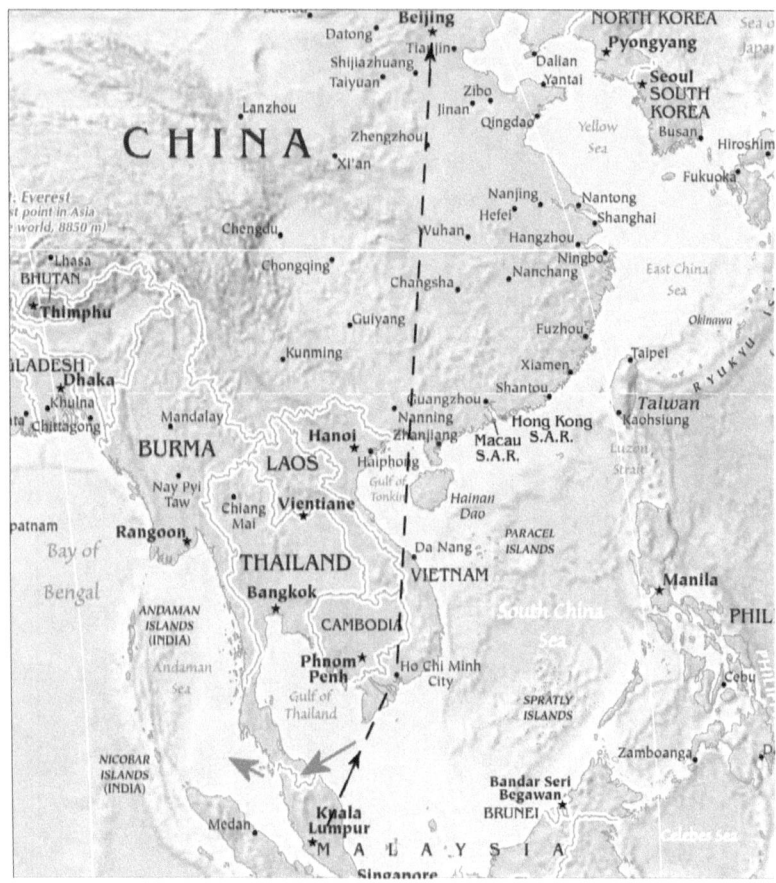

Broken pointers show intended path in Vietnam & China airspace; dark arrows show diversion over Gulf of Thailand, new direction due west, then possibly northwest (arguable from last flight data, TBD).

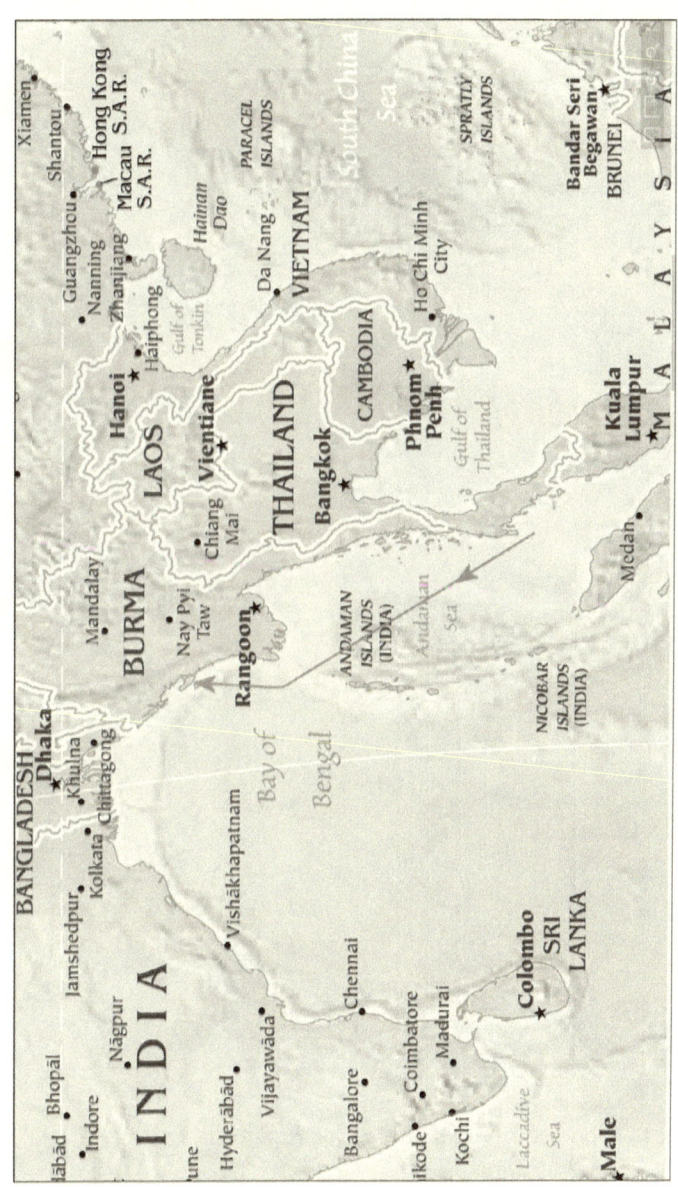

Hypothetical flight path Penang region to Ramree Isl. Burma.

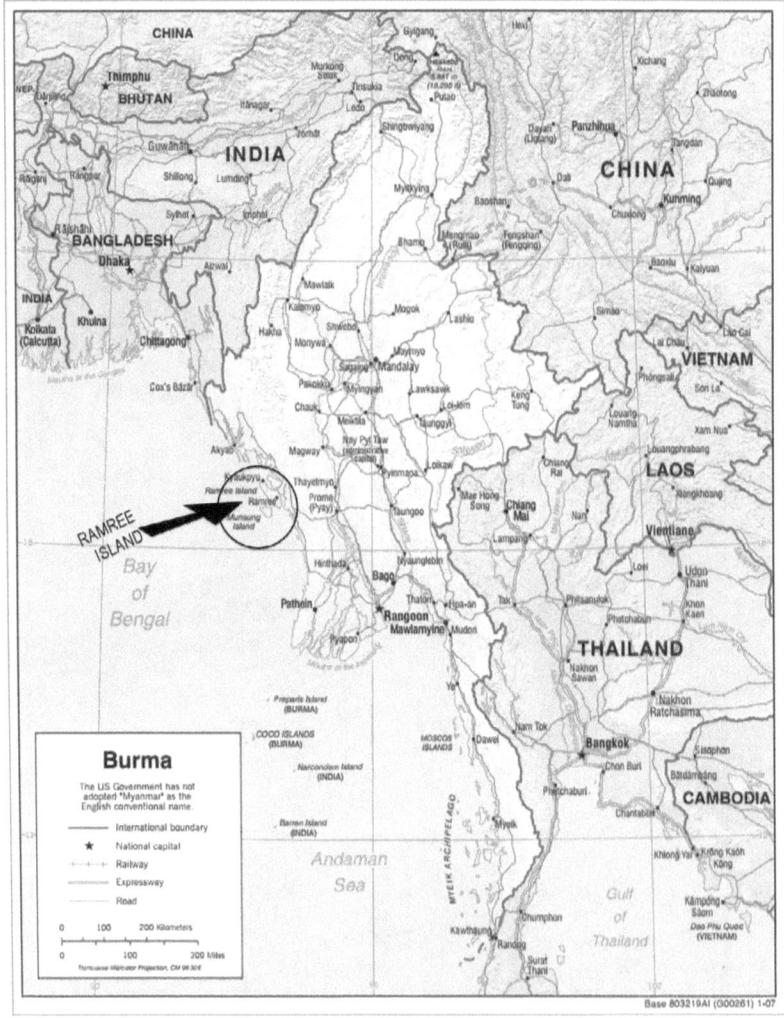

Pointer to hypothetical refitting place on Ramree Island.

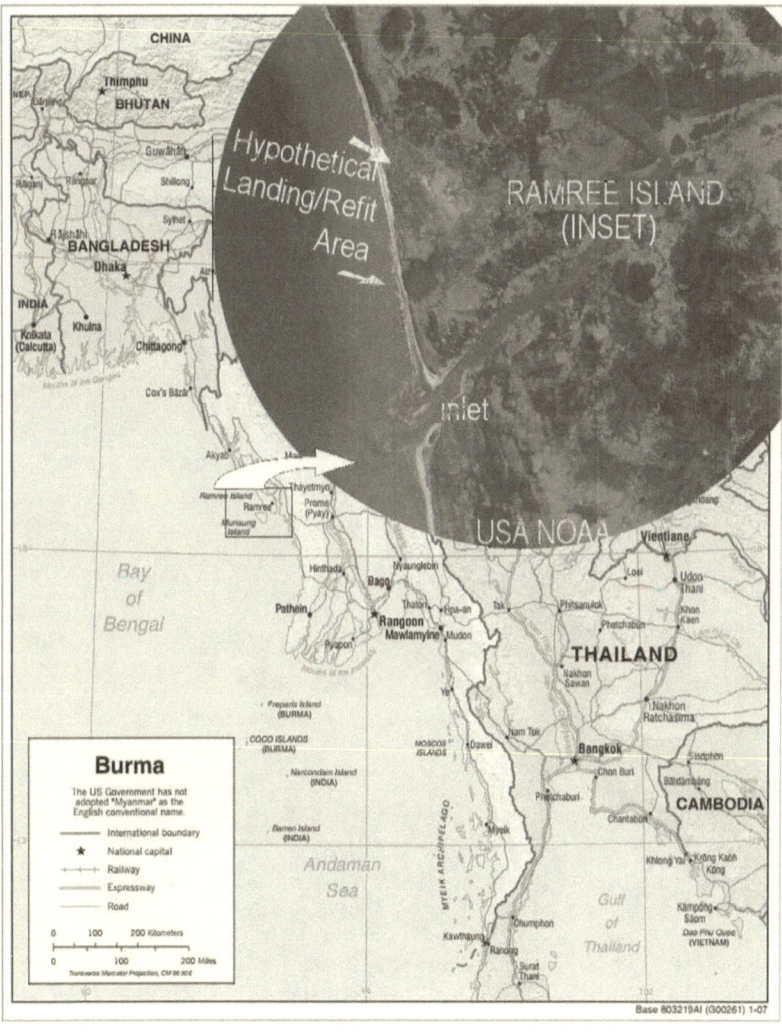

Pointer to hypothetical refitting place on Ramree Island with inset detail.

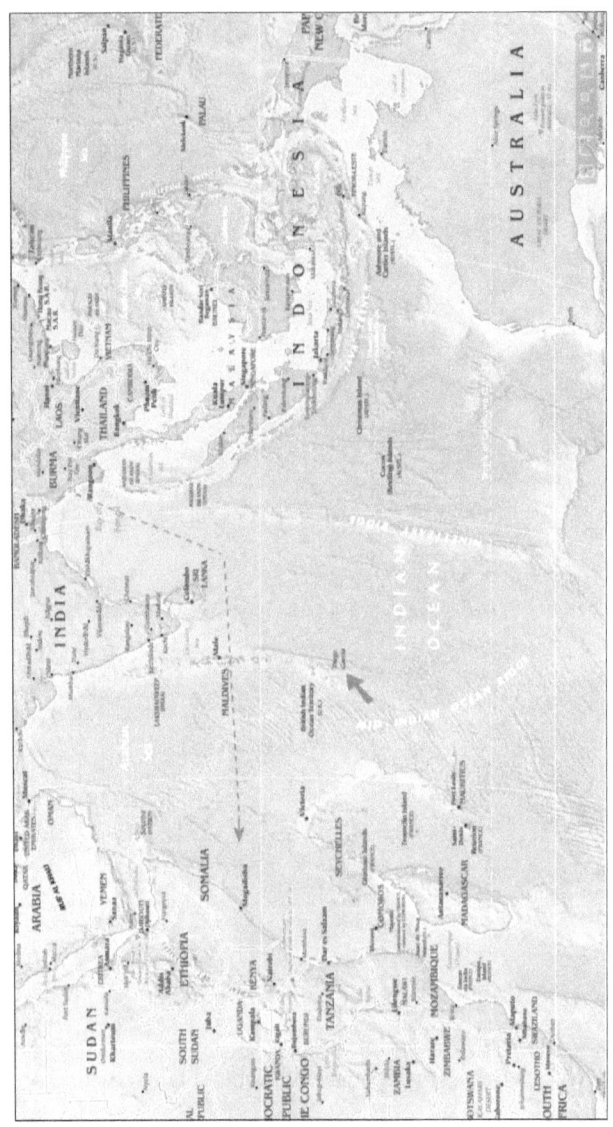

Hypothetical flight path Ramree Island, south of Sri Lanka, through Maldives chain, toward Africa. Note Seychelles, where Ilois (Chagossians) resettled as well as on Mauritius in 1960s.

33.   British Indian Ocean Territories with Diego Garcia

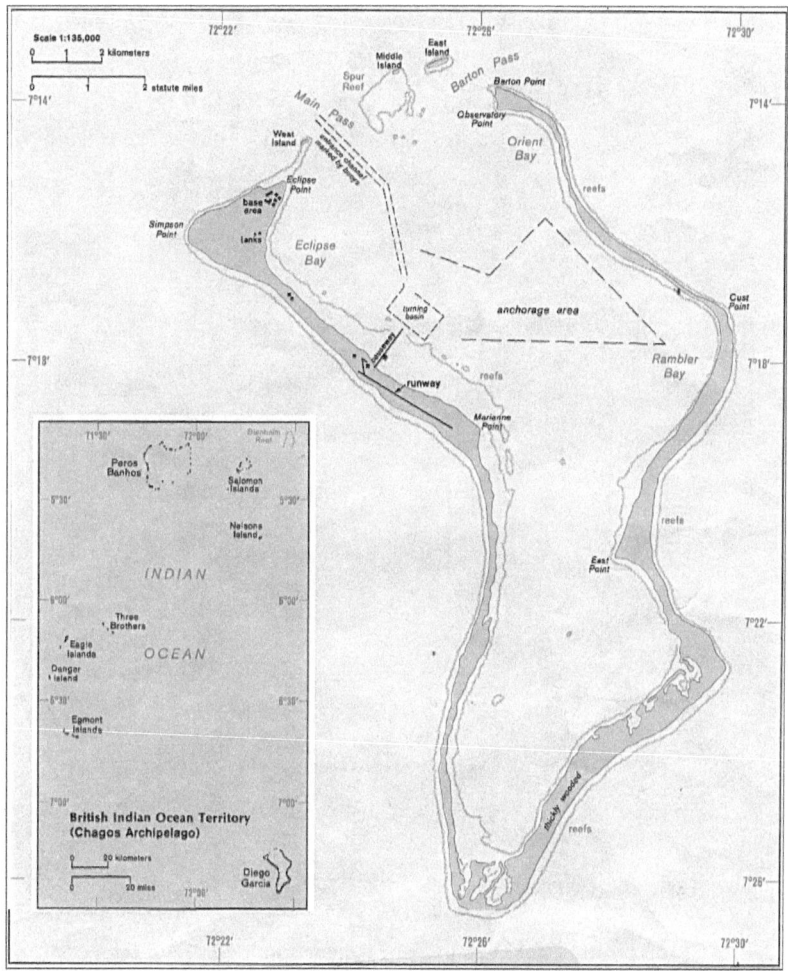

Diego Garcia atoll (BIOT) leased by U.S., largest land mass in BIOT. Turtle Bay at bottom, major double airstrip center left ('runway'), base top left, plantation around East Point area. Note 3 islands in entrance to lagoon. Perimeter about 40 miles (64 km); lagoon is 13 mi (21 km) N/S by up to 7 mi (11 km) E/W at N.

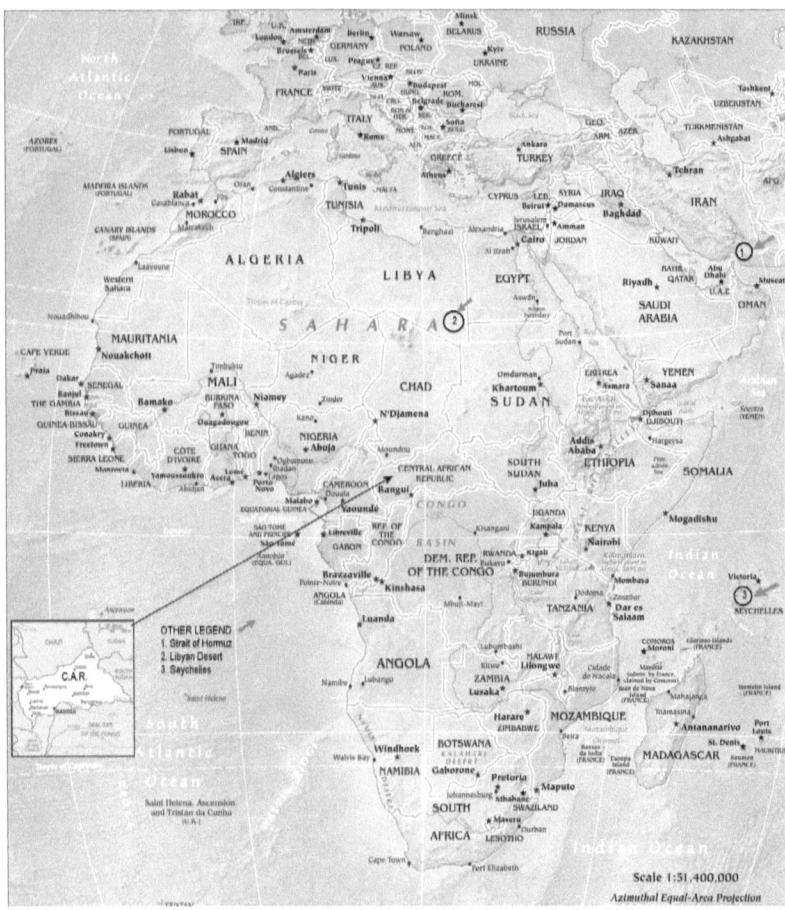

C.A.R. (inset) hypothetical Camp Zero is near south center of the country.
I have given flight distances re: Khartoum, Sudan; hiding a the 777 at (2)
in Libya might affect flight times slightly by +/- 1 hr. Inset points are (1)
Strait of Hormuz; (2) Great Sand Sea; (3) Seychelles off E coast of Africa.

About Clocktower Books

Clocktower Books maintains an active publishing program based on quality rather than quantity. Submissions currently are by invitation only. See the website at www.clocktowerbooks.com/.

Clocktower Books in 1996 published history's two first complete, proprietary (not public domain) e-books for download from the World Wide Web. These were *Neon Blue* by John Argo (Suspense) and *Heartbreaker* by John Argo (later retitled *This Shoal of Space* and currently marketed as *Cold Bright: Zoë Calla & the Dark Starship*).

A third original SF novel, *Pioneers* by John Argo, followed in 1997. Clocktower Books has been an innovator in digital publishing since its launch as The Haunted Village, Neon Blue Fiction, and Clocktower Fiction. A significant amount of this history has been preserved in such media as the Wayback Machine.

Clocktower Books published what was for nearly a decade the world's oldest professional, Web-only magazine of SF&F in accordance with SFWA rules, named *Outside: Speculative & Dark Fiction*, later *Deep Outside SFFH*, and ultimately *Far Sector SFFH*. We published many new writers as well as contemporary and later recipients of, and nominees for major prizes including Hugo and Nebula Awards. Museum information is at the Clocktower Books website (www.clocktowerbooks.com/) and at the magazine websites (www.deepoutside.com and www.farsector.com).

About the Author

John T. Cullen is an author who travels widely in the European Union, Canada, and the United States. He holds Bachelor degrees in English and Computer Information Systems, and a Master's in Business Administration from Boston University. He is married, with one son and one cat, and lives in Southern California. He served in the U.S. Army in West Germany during the Cold War. He writes full time, across a wide spectrum of fiction and nonfiction topics. He has written literary works, historical suspense (The Spy's Daughter), at least one important political thriller (The Generals of October, about a possible coup resulting from a Second Constitutional Convention), and the Empire of Time SF series (still in development). On the nonfiction side, his works include A Walk in Ancient Rome (a virtual tour of the ancient capital circa 300 CE) and Dead Move (first ever plausible analysis of the 1892 true crime at the Hotel del Coronado near San Diego). His personal website is www.johntcullen.com/.